William Jessup University
Paul Nystrom Library
333 Sunset Blvd.
Rocklin, CA, 95765

GRAPHIC DESIGN

by Stuart A. Kallen

LUCENT BOOKS
A part of Gale, Cengage Learning

GALE
CENGAGE Learning

Detroit • New York • San Francisco • New Haven, Conn • Waterville, Maine • London

LIBRARY OF CONGRESS CATALOGING-IN-PUBLICATION DATA

Kallen, Stuart A., 1955–
  Graphic design / by Stuart A. Kallen.
     p. cm. -- (Eye on art)
  Includes bibliographical references and index.
  ISBN 978-1-4205-0044-8 (hardcover)
  1. Graphic arts--History. I. Title.
  NC998.K35 2009
  741.6--dc22

                                                2008045441

Lucent Books
27500 Drake Rd.
Farmington Hills, MI 48331

ISBN-13: 978-1-4205-0044-8
ISBN-10: 1-4205-0044-9

Printed in the United States of America
2 3 4 5 6 7 13 12 11 10 09

CONTENTS

Foreword

"Art has no other purpose than to brush aside . . . everything that veils reality from us in order to bring us face to face with reality itself."

—French philosopher Henri-Louis Bergson

Some thirty-one thousand years ago, early humans painted strikingly sophisticated images of horses, bison, rhinoceroses, bears, and other animals on the walls of a cave in southern France. The meaning of these elaborate pictures is unknown, although some experts speculate that they held ceremonial significance. Regardless of their intended purpose, the Chauvet-Pont-d'Arc cave paintings represent some of the first known expressions of the artistic impulse.

From the Paleolithic era to the present day, human beings have continued to create works of visual art. Artists have developed painting, drawing, sculpture, engraving, and many other techniques to produce visual representations of landscapes, the human form, religious and historical events, and countless other subjects. The artistic impulse also finds expression in glass, jewelry, and new forms inspired by new technology. Indeed, judging by humanity's prolific artistic output throughout history, one must conclude that the compulsion to produce art is an inherent aspect of being human, and the results are among humanity's greatest cultural achievements: masterpieces such as the architectural marvels of ancient Greece, Michelangelo's perfectly rendered statue *David*, Vincent van Gogh's visionary painting *Starry Night*, and endless other treasures.

The creative impulse serves many purposes for society. At its most basic level, art is a form of entertainment or the means for a satisfying or pleasant aesthetic experience. But art's true power lies not in its potential to entertain and delight but in its ability to enlighten, to reveal the truth, and by doing so to uplift the human spirit and transform the human race.

One of the primary functions of art has been to serve religion. For most of Western history, for example, artists were paid by the church to produce works with religious themes and subjects. Art was thus a tool to help human beings transcend mundane, secular reality and achieve spiritual enlightenment. One of the best-known, and largest-scale, examples of Christian religious art is the Sistine Chapel in the Vatican in Rome. In 1508 Pope Julius II commissioned Italian Renaissance artist Michelangelo to paint the chapel's vaulted ceiling, an area of 640 square yards (535 sq. m). Michelangelo spent four years on scaffolding, his neck craned, creating a panoramic fresco of some three hundred human figures. His paintings depict Old Testament prophets and heroes, sibyls of Greek mythology, and nine scenes from the Book of Genesis, including the Creation of Adam, the Fall of Adam and Eve from the Garden of Eden, and the Flood. The ceiling of the Sistine Chapel is considered one of the greatest works of Western art and has inspired the awe of countless Christian pilgrims and other religious seekers. As eighteenth-century German poet and author Johann Wolfgang von Goethe wrote, "Until you have seen this Sistine Chapel, you can have no adequate conception of what man is capable of."

In addition to inspiring religious fervor, art can serve as a force for social change. Artists are among the visionaries of any culture. As such, they often perceive injustice and wrongdoing and confront others by reflecting what they see in their work. One classic example of art as social commentary was created in May 1937, during the brutal Spanish civil war. On May 1 Spanish artist Pablo Picasso learned of the recent attack on the small Basque village of Guernica by German airplanes allied with fascist forces led by Francisco Franco. The German pilots had used the village for target practice, a three-hour bombing that killed sixteen hundred civilians. Picasso, living in Paris, channeled his outrage over the massacre into his painting *Guernica*, a black, white, and gray mural that depicts dismembered animals and fractured human figures whose faces are contorted in agonized expressions. Initially, critics and the public condemned the painting as an incoherent hodgepodge, but the work soon came to be seen as a powerful antiwar statement and remains an iconic symbol of the violence and terror that dominated world events during the remainder of the twentieth century.

The impulse to create art—whether painting animals with crude pigments on a cave wall, sculpting a human form from marble, or commemorating human tragedy in a mural—thus serves many purposes. It offers an entertaining diversion, nourishes the imagination and the spirit, decorates and beautifies the world, and chronicles the age. But underlying all these functions is the desire to reveal that which is obscure—to illuminate, clarify, and perhaps ennoble. As Picasso himself stated, "The purpose of art is washing the dust of daily life off our souls."

The Eye on Art series is intended to assist readers in understanding the various roles of art in society. Each volume offers an in-depth exploration of a major artistic movement, medium, figure, or profession. All books in the series are beautifully illustrated with full-color photographs and diagrams. Riveting narrative, clear technical explanation, informative sidebars, fully documented quotes, a bibliography, and a thorough index all provide excellent starting points for research and discussion. With these features, the Eye on Art series is a useful introduction to the world of art—a world that can offer both insight and inspiration.

Introduction

Communicating a Message

The act of combining words and pictures to convey a message has many names. It has been referred to as graphic design, visual communication, design expression, commercial art, and graphic art. But whatever it is called, it is everywhere. People are bombarded with graphic designs from the moment they look at the trademark on their alarm clock in the morning until they put their computer to sleep at night. They see graphic art on their coffee cups, T-shirts, handbags, cell phones, automobiles, highway signs, and on countless advertisements. Even people traipsing through the wilderness or climbing mountains are carrying visual communications in the form of trademarks on their hiking boots, Global Positioning Systems, cell phones, backpacks, and tents. Graphic designs are so ubiquitous that they hardly attract notice. But the graphic arts that are so much a part of modern culture have a long lineage that can be traced back centuries. From the first book publishers in the Middle Ages to the creators of twenty-first-century computer icons, graphic designers have profoundly transformed the way people see the world.

In its earliest days, graphic art was based on an integration of art, craft, business, science, technology, and language. In the fifteenth century, the science of ink and paper production was melded with the technology of the printing press. This created the business of book production, in which graphic artists combined art and language. In the nineteenth century, science and technology led to the invention of the lithographic press, the camera, and the photogravure reproduction process. These developments spawned a mass-media revolution that was driven by eye-catching graphic designs. Today Web designers continue to rely on art, craft, business, science, technology, and language to create cutting-edge Web sites and video games.

A McDonald's restaurant sign in Moscow, Russia. Its trademark "golden arches" are an internationally recognized graphic design.

Visual Poetry

However artful their products may be, graphic designers are not considered fine artists like painters and sculptors. Because most graphic art relies on words and text as well as pictures and illustrations, graphic designs are generally considered communication rather than art. And while fine artists often rely on obscure symbolism that can be interpreted in numerous ways, it is usually required that graphic artists communicate messages clearly so that they can be understood by nearly everyone.

That is not to say that the art aspect cannot be emphasized in graphic design. In fact, some of the great art movements of the past century, such as modernism, art deco, and cubism, found their way into graphic arts. By incorporating these styles into their work, graphic artists rejected the division between fine art and commercial art. In doing so, they created a visual poetry that inventively melds words and images into clever and aesthetically pleasing messages. Like any good art, quality graphic arts can fuel the imagination.

While the majority of graphic art is used for mundane communications, lasting designs have become part of the social fabric. For example, the Coca-Cola logo is instantly recognized in nearly every country on Earth. Logos for other companies, such as Apple, Mercedes Benz, and McDonald's, are similarly well-known. Although some have despaired that children recognize a soft-drink logo before a painting by Leonardo da Vinci, that is the nature of graphic art.

Leonardo might have used his paints to incorporate dozens of symbols into a single painting that viewers could contemplate anew down through the centuries. But Coca-Cola wants to sell its product to people in America, Armenia, and Afghanistan. And a simple piece of graphic art has allowed them to communicate this message to billions of people speaking thousands of languages in hundreds of countries throughout the world.

Everyday Art

When most people think of communication, they think of speech or words on a page or screen. But the art of graphics is based on communicating ideas quickly, clearly, and concisely. To achieve these goals, graphic artists have developed efficient ways to communicate based on symbols, trademarks, and picture images called pictographs or pictograms. Some of these icons are universally recognized to represent something, and others are cryptic; that is, they only have meaning to a certain group of people. Whatever the purpose, these graphic designs represent a basic form of art that is nearly everywhere in daily life.

The most basic unit of visual communication is the symbol, a simple picture that represents a concept, an idea, or information. One of the most recognized symbols is the red circle with a slash through the middle. This is understood to mean "do not" or "no" in almost every nation on Earth. A common example is seen when a picture image, or pictogram, of a cigarette is inserted into the red circle, designating a no-smoking area.

Symbols that represent religious beliefs are also understood by billions of people. Common religious symbols include the Christian cross, the six-point star of Judaism, and the crescent moon with a five-point star that identifies Islam. These symbols

The "No-Smoking" graphic uses one of the most recognized symbols for "do not" or "no": a circle with a slash through it.

have been used for centuries to define houses of worship, the content of books, and the faith of people who wear them as ornaments such as necklaces and rings.

Other common visual symbols are the letters of alphabets. Letters are symbols that represent sounds formed by the mouth and tongue. While letters may be drawn differently or pronounced differently in various languages, they serve as a universal means for turning human ideas into visual communication through words.

Pictograms, Ideograms, and Logograms

Symbols are a basic unit of visual communication, but they can be used to convey complex words, concepts, ideas, and actions. Therefore, a variety of symbols has been developed that express ideas, concepts, words, or phrases. Rebuses are pictures that represent a person's name. However, sometimes the boundaries between pictograms, ideograms, and logograms are not clearly defined, and the words are used interchangeably. Whatever they are called, these symbols have been common throughout the development of human civilization and remain so today.

Pictograms represent objects and were first drawn on cave walls in Africa and Europe more than thirty thousand years ago. The simple symbols that have survived represent bison, deer, birds, and the sun. Drawings also include stick figures that symbolize people, villages, and hunters holding shields and spears. Anthropologists speculate that these early graphic communications were either used as magical symbols in religious rites or simply as way to leave a message about hunting prospects to those who followed. Whatever their exact purpose, the images in the prehistoric pictograms are still understood by people three hundred centuries after they were drawn.

Pictograms called ideograms represent more complex concepts. The most common ideograms are numbers. For example, the numeral 5 represents the idea of five units and can be used to quantify anything from apples to asteroids.

One popular ideogram, the heart symbol, ♥, stands for the complex concept of love. In the world of advertising, the ideogram "I ♥ NY" ("I love New York"), created by legendary graphic designer Milton Glaser, was a breakthrough that has been imitated countless times. Such simple designs have become

The ideogram "I ♥ New York" is a simple design that has been imitated many times.

critical in advertising at a time when many cities and corporations are marketing themselves to people all over the world.

While ideograms symbolize concepts, logograms represent entire words or phrases. A simple logogram, the ampersand (&), is the sign that represents the word *and*. In more complex forms, the written Chinese language is composed of fifty thousand characters that combine logograms, ideograms, and pictograms. In Chinese writing, pictograms shaped like a crescent moon represent the moon. Ideograms in the shape of a T or inverted T are used to express concepts that mean "above" or "below." Logograms are drawn when entire words need to be expressed. Taken together, Chinese characters are highly stylized pictures that express words, phrases, ideas, feelings, colors, actions, sizes, and types of objects.

Dollars and Symbols

In the United States, the one dollar bill is packed with pictograms and ideograms. But the symbols on it are either ignored or misunderstood by many Americans.

One of the most enduring symbols on the dollar is the Great Seal of the United States. The symbol's creation was decreed by the Continental Congress on July 4, 1776, the same day that the Declaration of Independence was signed. But it took nearly six years and numerous revisions by graphic artists before the symbol was adopted. And the meaning of the Great Seal has been debated for more than two centuries since Benjamin Franklin, John Adams, and Thomas Jefferson first proposed the design.

The front of the Great Seal shows ideograms of an American eagle, a shield, an olive branch, and thirteen arrows. The eagle represents the idea of freedom. The shield stands for the concept of strength. And the arrows are symbolic of the thirteen original states. The arrows and the olive branch also represent war and peace. The back of the Great Seal, on the left side of the dollar, shows an unfinished or uncapped pyramid. Hovering above the symbol is the capstone, which, if lowered, would complete the pyramid. Inside the capstone is an eye, called the Eye of Providence, surrounded by rays of light. The

U.S. Treasury Department provides the official meaning of the symbols: "The unfinished pyramid means that the United States will always grow, improve and build. . . . [The] 'All-Seeing Eye' located above the pyramid suggests the importance of divine guidance in favor of the American cause."[1]

While few people bother to look closely at their money as they spend it, these ideograms have created controversy over the centuries. Some have concluded that the symbols are occult icons that represent an ancient secret society called the Freemasons. The symbols are sometimes interpreted to mean that the Founding Fathers were Freemasons who wanted to impose a tyrannical new world order on the people of the United States. Although Freemasons in the modern fraternal organization deny this falsehood, it has been repeated continually for centuries and remains a featured topic on several conspiracy-related Web sites.

Coats of Arms

The controversy over the symbols on the dollar bill prove how powerful graphic designs can be. This was understood by medieval artists who created designs called coats of arms to represent knights, nobles, and influential families. The symbols used on these complex graphic creations were meant to inspire fear, respect, and awe in the people who viewed them.

The Great Seal on an American dollar bill is a complex ideogram.

In modern times coats of arms are seen on product logos, dinnerware, and the letterheads of colleges and universities. Any designer wishing to grant an air of regal lineage or status to a product can use a coat of arms for that purpose. But in centuries past, a coat of arms was a highly respected symbol that

A NEW PROFESSION

In the early twentieth century, improved methods of production and communication created a culture increasingly based on consumerism. This required a growing number of skilled graphic artists to work for printers and publishers, as British design historian Jeremy Aynsley explains in A Century of Graphic Design:

Graphic design was a new profession for a new century. Its emergence was underpinned by major technological changes. . . . For the modern communications system to emerge an infrastructure of mechanized printing, ink and paper manufacture and specialist machinery for folding, binding and stapling was necessary. This was prompted by a huge change in the pattern of life of urban populations. . . . The migration of people to towns and cities to find industrialized work, the growth of railway networks and the steady increase in the mass market for consumer goods were linked to other important changes. Modern communications became dependent on reproduction, at first through print and later in the century through radio, television and film. Books, magazines, posters and advertisements began to be produced on an unprecedented scale, for instruction, education and entertainment. This led . . . to the concentration of large-scale printing houses in cities.

The responsibility to train young workers for the graphic trades and industries had previously belonged to the guilds, but now trade schools and colleges of art and design took on the task. . . . Matters of taste and aesthetics were taught alongside technical skills. An understanding of [decoration] was considered fundamental to all branches of design and the best way to reform taste.

Jeremy Aynsley, *A Century of Graphic Design.* Hauppauge, NY: Barron's Educational Series, 2001, p. 14.

was passed from father to eldest son. And the uses of the coat of arms were governed by strict laws.

The word *heraldry* came into used in the twelfth century to define the art of creating a coat of arms. Those who practiced heraldry originally designed coats of arms to be displayed on helmets, chest armor, or shields of knights. A coat of arms would identify a knight when he participated in battles. A knight would also display the symbols on armor and banners when competing in tournaments that featured mock combat between opponents. The importance of the coat of arms in these sporting events is explained on the Fleur-de-lis Designs Web page: "[Coats] of arms became military status symbols, and their popularity increased along with the popularity of the tournament. . . . The tournament became a training ground for knights, and its pageantry became more elaborate as time passed. Some knights made their living (and their reputations) roaming from tournament to tournament."[2]

In these tournaments a well-known coat of arms was like an advertisement for the bearer. It informed spectators of the knight's character, qualifications, and lineage. These were expressed by the basic elements of the coat that included the shield, the mantling, the helmet (or helm), images called charges, and the crest.

The shield was the central element on the coat of arms and resembled metal shields used for protection in battle. A shield may contain charges (images) such as the traditional lion or a lily flower design called a fleur-de-lis. Other charges included a chevron for protection, a crown designating royal authority, or a hydra (a dragon with seven heads), which meant the bearer had conquered a very powerful enemy. Background colors on the shield also imparted meaning. Blue was symbolic of truth and loyalty. Gold spoke of generosity, and red informed viewers that the knight was a warrior with great military strength.

The shield was surrounded by a graphic design called mantling. This often combined vines or leaves, animals such as unicorns and stags, and the helm, a drawing of a knight's helmet. Like other design elements, the mantling symbols informed observers of the bearer's heritage, character, and accomplishments.

The Glasgow coat of arms shows the different elements of a coat of arms, including the shield at the center, the mantling around the shield, the helm above the shield, and the crest above the helmet.

The crest was displayed above the shield and was so named because it often appeared standing alone atop the drawing of a knight's helmet. Lions were popular animals included on crests, but the symbols could also include a hand holding a weapon or the upper torso of a person. In Germany crest designs such as a tall hat or plume of feathers were common. In England knights' crests might show a bull horn with flowers protruding from the end. Whatever the crest, it was often seen as a symbol representing the family name. Coats of arms still displayed by the Vatican and European nobles can be traced back eight hundred years or more. The Japanese equivalent, called *kamon*, have been used by some families for more than thirteen centuries. Perhaps one of the most famous Japanese *kamon*, the Mitsubishi logo represented by three triangles, has its roots in an ancient family of warriors called the Tosa clan. Another coat of arms associated with automobiles may be found on Porsches. This badge is the coat of arms of the city of Stuttgart, where the cars are made. The rearing horse in the center of the shield honors the ancient horse-breeding farm where the Porsche factory was built. The antlers and red and black stripes are taken from the coat of arms representing the kingdom of Württemberg, now part of Germany, where Stuttgart is located.

Monograms

Like coats of arms, the use of monograms was once restricted to nobility, but today they are found on numerous consumer products. Monograms are simply graphic designs that contain one or more letters that represent the initials of the bearer. Usually, the initials are overlapped or intertwined into a single symbol, with elements such as leaves or vines added to create a pleasing appearance.

Monograms may be seen on some of the most expensive designer goods, but they first came into use because of widespread ignorance and illiteracy. In ancient times kings who could not read had monograms designed with the letters of their initials. When a king was presented with official documents, read to him by a lawyer or priest, he would affix his monogram to the papers instead of signing his name.

In more recent years, monograms came to be associated with trendy fashion designers. This began after luggage maker Louis Vuitton started placing a monogrammed LV on his products in the early twentieth century to battle counterfeiters who were making cheap imitations of his quality baggage. Vuitton's practical idea turned into a fashion fad, according to Learn AboutHandbags.com: "[Any] handbags or purses that carry this initial [are] an ultimate must-have to celebrities, to the rich and famous, and even to the middle class fashion aspirants."[3]

And the fashion conscious are willing to pay extra for their status symbols—a pair of sunglasses bearing the Roberto Cavalli monogram sell for $390, while generic sunglasses of similar quality may be purchased for around $50.

Bricks and Books

Designer trademarks also add value to a product. And like monograms and coats of arms, trademarks have roots in ancient history. But today trademarks are pasted on nearly everything in a modern home, including baby toys, T-shirts, televisions, and kitchen appliances.

Technically, trademarks are any marks or signs affixed to a product that identify its origin. These marks first appeared on bricks and roof tiles in Mesopotamia and Egypt more than three thousand years ago. During the days of ancient Rome, more than two thousand years ago, trademarks on bricks contained unusual symbols that identified the county where the bricks were made, the manufacturer's name, the estate where the clay was found, the building contractor, and even the name of the emperor. These trademarks were probably created for tax purposes—they listed everyone who profited from the production of the brick. However, they have left historians with an interesting record of Roman life. For example, the prevalence of female names on the trademarks indicates that women were operating heavy construction businesses in ancient times.

In later centuries trademarks appeared on tiles, pottery, and hand-carved building stones. After the invention of the printing press in the fifteenth century, publishers began putting their personal symbols, called colophons, on their books. Because many books were considered works of art in the mid-1400s, colophons began as a way for a printer to sign the work, much as an artist would sign a painting. Within a century, colophons were printed or hand stamped in color on nearly every book.

Many of the symbols were based on what was called the orb and cross. This design was created from a circle and a cross featuring a double bar. This simple design was the basis for hundreds of creative graphics that included the printer's monogram and other stylized drawings in the circle.

MINIATURE WORLDS

In Trademarks of the '60s and '70s, *communications professor Philip B. Meggs describes the importance of modern trademarks:*

Trademarks are the linchpins of contemporary communication. These small graphic designs signify a particular cola drink, television network, or manufacturer. They differentiate each company, product, or service from its competitors. Trademarks become miniature worlds that store memories, passions, and reputations in the minds of employees, customers, and stockholders. From corner restaurants to multinational corporations whose activities circumnavigate a shrinking planet, every organization has to have one. These crown jewels of business are the most public and recognizable faces of far-flung conglomerates.

Each decade a new army of trademarks marches forth to join the thousands already in use. Many new trademarks survive the mercurial fashions of their day and become part of our stable of familiar icons. At the same time hundreds of trademarks are forced into retirement as companies go out of business, replace an obsolete trademark with a more contemporary design or vanish in a leveraged buyout or merger.

Quoted in Tyler Blik, *Trademarks of the '60s and '70s.* San Francisco: Chronicle, 1998, p. 8.

A Visual Shortcut

As the centuries passed, trademarks became less complicated and mysterious. By the late nineteenth century, there were a growing number of manufacturers, and each was striving to distinguish itself in the marketplace. Trademark designers were faced with the task of conveying the type of product, the producer, and the nature of the business in the shortest way possible. To do so, they designed trademarks, also called logos, which would be used on labels, bottles, letterheads, advertisements, and signs.

This intensely human picture
stands for all that is best in music

RCA's logo of a Jack Russell terrier listening to an old-style phonograph represents the golden age of trademark design.

This resulted in a golden age of trademark design, some of which are still recognizable today. Two examples produced in the late 1880s are the Rock of Gibraltar symbol used for Prudential Insurance Company and the RCA logo of a Jack Russell terrier listening to an old-style phonograph.

By the twentieth century it was an established notion that any business hoping for lasting success needed a memorable trademark. In *Seven Designers Look at Trademark Design*, Austrian graphic artist Herbert Bayer explains the qualities of a good trademark:

> The aim of [the trademark] . . . is to catch *attention*, to create *interest*, to be pleasing and attractive for *aesthetic* and *psychological* reasons, to *persuade* the observer to

buy. In achieving this, the idea of consciously or subconsciously remembering the . . . message is of greatest importance. Here is where a well conceived trademark properly used will function best. A good mark is a visual shortcut with the special property of remaining recognized after it has once made a place for itself in the world of symbols.[4]

The Birth of the Corporate Identity

With so much importance attached to a relatively simple piece of graphics, perhaps it is not surprising that some of the most talented designers were hired by companies to create corporate artwork. Some of these artists designed logos and labels, while others expanded their horizons to create furniture, wallpaper, textiles, and architectural designs. German graphic arts pioneer Peter Behrens produced it all.

Behrens studied painting as a young man but by 1900 became interested in the designs of the arts and crafts movement. Based in Great Britain, proponents of the arts and crafts style stood in opposition to the shoddy, mass-produced goods of the Victorian era. The founders of the movement valued styles based on beautiful designs that could be created by skilled craftspeople, who were increasingly unemployable during the factory era. As movement founder William Morris stated, arts and crafts products were created "for the people and by the people, and a source of pleasure to the maker and the user."[5]

Inspired by Morris's words, Behrens designed a villa in Darmstadt in 1902 based on the arts and crafts movement. The building was considered a *Gesamtkunstwerk*, or total work of art, because Behrens not only produced the architectural drawings but also designed the furniture, towels, paintings, pottery, and dishes.

Five years after his arts and crafts success, Behrens went to work as artistic director for the German electronics company AEG. The company was a major manufacturer of generators, electric cables, lightbulbs, and arc lamps. While AEG was not considered a glamorous company, as Jeremy Aynsley writes in *A Century of Graphic Design*, "this was among the most celebrated appointments in design history, as it heralded the birth of the corporate identity."[6]

At first Behrens designed pamphlets, advertisements, and displays for international trade exhibitions. In 1908, however, he redesigned the corporate trademark to resemble a hexagonal honeycomb with the letters *AEG* printed in the designer's own elegant type font, Behrens-Antiqua. The logo was uniformly applied to all AEG printed graphics, buildings, and ads. It was

LOEWY WINS A BET

Graphic artist Raymond Loewy created package designs and logos for many of America's most successful brands. The official Raymond Loewy Web site describes the story behind his famous design for Lucky Strike cigarettes:

[**L**oewy] began designing packaging and logos in 1940 when George Washington Hill, then president of the American Tobacco Company, wagered him $50,000 [equal to about $700,000 in 2008] that he could not improve the appearance of the already familiar green and red Lucky Strike cigarette package. Accepting the challenge, Loewy began by changing the package background from green to white, thereby reducing printing costs by eliminating the need for green dye. Next he placed the red Lucky Strike target on both sides of the package, increasing product visibility and ultimately product sales. A satisfied Hill paid off the bet, and for over 40 years the Lucky Strike pack has remained unchanged.

"I'm looking for a very high index of visual retention," Loewy explained of his logos. "We want anyone who has seen the logotype even fleetingly to never forget it."

Official Web Site of Raymond Loewy, "About: Biography." www.raymondloewy.com/about/bio2.html, 2008.

also stamped on the company's new products such as electric kettles, lamps, and fans. This was the first complete corporate identity scheme in graphic arts history, and as Aynsley writes, it "led to a visual consistency in all AEG goods, which brought instant recognition by the consumer. Extensive use of Behrens-Antiqua gave the company's identity a clean, sober appearance and brought AEG praise for its systematic ordering of product information."[7]

Behrens was also a teacher, and his students spread his ideas on design throughout Europe and North America. Today the public image of nearly every corporation has its roots in Behrens's concept of integrated graphic design.

Streamlining

Behrens was one of the first graphic designers to earn international recognition for his work. His success with AEG prompted ad agencies in the United States to recruit designers, fine artists, and illustrators who would create print ads and product packaging. These people were given job titles such as "consumer engineer" and "product stylist," and they were expected to generate demand for various products through the use of art and design.

Foremost among the consumer engineers was French-born illustrator Raymond Loewy, whose early work was inspired by the art deco movement. The term *art deco* originated in France in the mid-1920s and was characterized by illustrations of models with elongated torsos accompanied by geometric forms, sweeping curves, chevrons, and semicircular sunburst patterns meant to be elegant, stylish, and modern.

Loewy's career as an industrial designer began in 1929 when he was hired to change the look of the Gestetner copy machine. Loewy changed the look of the mundane machine by smoothing its shape and giving it the appearance of an object that moved swiftly like an airplane or submarine, a design style called streamlining.

During the following four decades, Loewy streamlined hundreds of products, including toothbrushes, electric razors, the two-story Greyhound Scenic Cruiser bus, locomotives, and even the interiors of the Saturn and Skylab spacecrafts. In his efforts to streamline automobiles in the late 1940s, Loewy introduced now-standard design elements such as slanted windshields, built-in headlights, wheel covers, and lower, slimmer body designs. A classic example is the Loewy-designed 1953 Studebaker with a long nose. The car looked like it was moving quickly even when parked.

In the world of visual communications, Loewy redesigned the label and package for Lucky Strike cigarettes and streamlined the Coca-Cola bottle. He created logos for Exxon, Shell, Frigidaire, Nabisco, and the U.S. Postal Service. It is said that by 1951, a person could spend his or her entire day using products with graphics and designs styled by Raymond Loewy Associates. Commenting on the incessant demand for his work, Loewy wrote, "We were able to convince some creative men that good appearance was a salable commodity, that it often cut costs, enhanced a product's prestige, raised corporate profits, benefited the customer and increased employment."[8]

Raymond Loewy's corporate designs and logos permeated mid- to late-twentieth-century culture. Many of his designs, such as the Shell Gas logo shown here, are still instantly recognizable.

Loewy died on July 14, 1986, at the age of ninety-two. The occasion was marked by an outpouring of tributes concerning his contributions to graphic and industrial design. In the *New York Times*, reporter Susan Heller summed up the feeling of many in the design world: "One can hardly open a beer or a soft drink, fix breakfast, board a plane, buy gas, mail a letter or shop for an appliance without encountering a Loewy creation."[9]

A Window into the Past

Designers like Loewy and Behrens became celebrities for their creative abilities, but countless anonymous graphic artists have influenced culture for generations. When looking at a dollar bill, an old *National Geographic*, or an antique soda bottle, graphic arts act as living history by providing a window into the past. And perhaps five hundred years from today, anthropologists will study Web sites, beer cans, and the latest music magazines in an attempt to understand the look and feel of the world in the early twenty-first century.

2

Book Arts

More than thirty-two hundred years ago, dead Egyptian kings were buried with manuscripts containing hymns and magical spells called *Books of the Dead*. These ancient scrolls used a combination of pictures and words to direct deceased rulers past a variety of demons to the safety of the afterlife. The artists who designed the manuscripts placed the text in flowing harmony with the illustrations. In some cases words were intermingled with pictures or placed separately in boxes, much like sidebars in modern books. With their pleasing yet functional appearance, the pages of the *Books of the Dead* are some of the oldest surviving examples of graphic art.

In the centuries that followed, manuscripts were created by various other means. But whether they were made by religious scholars, artisans, or printers on letterpresses, the art of the book has been driving graphic design innovations for centuries.

Illuminated Manuscripts

In 2007 over 3,000 books were published every day in the United States—about 110,000 titles annually. The books covered subjects such as art, cooking, entertainment, economics, business, computers, and history. Some books consisted of words in black ink printed on cheap paper; others were large and expensive with beautiful color pictures on glossy paper. Whatever the style, the books required the work of graphic artists who laid out pages, positioned pictures, designed attractive covers, and picked type fonts. Much of this work was carried out on computers. But long before the digital age, book artists performed these tasks with skilled hands and primitive tools.

The term *manuscript* is derived from the Latin *manu scriptus*, meaning "written by hand." And in Europe, all books were

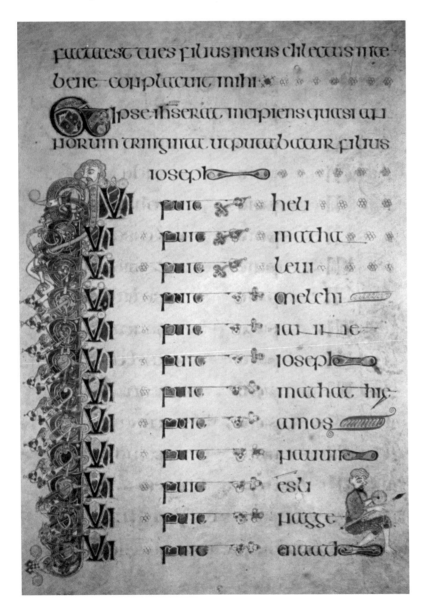

An illuminated manuscript from the *Book of Kells* shows an early example of graphic design.

handwritten until the advent of the printing press in the mid-fifteenth century. The earliest manuscripts were elaborately decorated religious works called codices (plural of codex), which consisted of folded sheets of paper secured between wooden boards. Most codices were created by Benedictine monks and were based on stories in the New Testament.

One of the oldest surviving codices is the *Book of Kells*. It features the four Gospels written in Latin. This elaborate and lavishly illustrated volume, called an illuminated manuscript, was created around A.D. 800 by Irish monks who combined art, graphics, and medieval bookmaking technology. Like ancient Egyptian scrolls, the graphic design of the book is interlinear, which means images are placed between the lines of text. And the text itself is embellished with an amazing array of decorated capital letters, borders, and small illustrations.

The *Book of Kells* is among thousands of illuminated manuscripts produced in Europe between the fifth and fifteenth centuries. While most were religious in nature, by the end of the Middle Ages, songbooks and books about biology, astronomy, and others sciences also appeared as illuminated manuscripts.

Graphic Arts in the Scriptorium

Illuminated manuscripts were often produced by monks who had the help of laypersons. Early graphic artists worked in a room dedicated to book production called a scriptorium—literally, "the place for writing." Because making a book by hand was a long, tedious process that could take a single individual at least six months, those working in scriptoria created manuscripts through a division of labor. With a team of workers possessing various skills, a copy could be created in about a month.

The first step in manuscript production involved cutting sheets of parchment to size. Lightly ruled lines were drawn on the paper by an apprentice. The basic layout was drawn in with silverpoint, a technique in which a graphic artist uses a pen with a tip of silver wire to draw a picture onto a piece of paper. The paper is coated with gesso, a mixture of chalk and rabbit-skin glue. As the picture is drawn, the gesso picks up delicate lines

of silver. Another artist, called a scribe, would laboriously write out the words of the book in beautiful script known as calligraphy. The completed pages were turned over to a highly skilled illuminator, who created painted images inside large letters at the beginning of each paragraph or page. These intricate letters with scenes painted in bright pigments are called majuscules.

After illuminators decorated the letters, border painters created a variety of pictures and ornamentations in page margins. These paintings are called miniatures, not for their small size but because of the use of a red pigment called *minum* in Latin. Commenting on the artistic quality of these pictures created in fifteenth-century Belgium, designer Norma Levarie writes in *The Art and History of Books*, "The border-painters evolved a new type of border to go with the realistic miniature: a flat broad band, usually of gold, strewn with the most tangible blossoms and insects, painted with artful . . . shadows that make one feel that one could pick them up off the page."[10]

Monks working in a scriptorium used division of labor to speed up the time-consuming process of producing a book.

After the pages were completed, another designer would lay out the graphics for the leather cover, which might be decorated with floral designs, crests, or religious scenes. These would be impressed or engraved into the leather with metal or wood stamps. For those who could afford it, the cover designs could be made in gold tooling, in which a thin layer of gold was applied by hand. The cover and pages of the final product were turned over to bookbinders, who sewed the pages together on one side to create a strong binding.

Large scriptoria in northern Europe employed dozens of workers to create several manuscripts at a time. The works combined text, imagery, and ornamentation into masterpieces

PEOPLE NEEDED BOOKS

In The Art and History of Books, *Norma Levarie describes how the scarcity of books affected life in fifteenth-century Europe:*

Copying manuscripts by hand was laborious and costly work. The books that existed were concentrated in the libraries of monasteries and universities, or in the rare private libraries that were the privilege of the very wealthy. A university such as Cambridge had only a hundred and twenty-two volumes in the year 1424. A private library at the end of the fifteenth century might boast of perhaps twenty volumes. A bound manuscript at that time cost as much money as an average court official received in a month. A scholar or student who was not exceptionally wealthy could only acquire books by copying them himself. The typical manuscript of the Middle Ages was not the splendid ornamented volume we know from reproductions or exhibitions; it was a hastily written copy made for practical use. In this time of scarcity . . . [people] needed books, and this need perhaps more than anything else brought about the beginning of printing.

Norma Levarie, *The Art and History of Books.* Newcastle, DE: Oak Knoll, 1995, p. 67.

that were landmarks in visual communications. Reading was made easier by graphic design elements such as headings, punctuation, and capital letters.

Wood-Block Books

Illuminated manuscripts were artistic masterpieces that were expensive and rare. But average Europeans rarely saw a book unless it was displayed in their church. However, around 1425 a technique imported from China and Japan called wood-block printing made books available to the masses for the first time.

Block printing involved sketching images and text, in reverse, onto blocks of beech wood. Expert woodcutters then carved the images into the blocks with chisels, knives, and files. The raised words and pictures were coated with ink and pressed onto paper.

Many wood-block books were filled with simple pictures and a few words to provide religious instruction and reading lessons to the illiterate. But others were masterpieces of graphic design. Illustrations were surrounded by columns and pillars that looked like elaborate sculptures commonly carved onto church walls and public buildings. Short phrases of text appeared inside banners and ribbons to attract the eye.

The art of block books reached its pinnacle in 1493 with the publication of *The Nuremberg Chronicle*. This work, a pictorial history of the earth from creation to the 1490s, was illustrated and engraved by Michael Wohlgemuth, Wilhelm Pleydenwurff, and renowned artist Albrecht Dürer. *The Nuremberg Chronicle*, printed in Nuremberg, Germany, contains 1,809 prints made from 645 wood blocks. The illustrations show religious scenes, villages, landscapes, everyday life, skeletons dancing, and people playing music.

Although *The Nuremberg Chronicle* took three years to produce, like all block books, only about fifty copies could be made from a set of blocks because the wood wore out quickly. Despite the intense labor required to carve dozens of sets of blocks, between 1493 and 1509 about fifteen hundred copies

Wood-block illustration of skeletons dancing from *The Nuremberg Chronicle.*

of *The Nuremberg Chronicle* were produced in Latin, while approximately nine hundred were printed in German. About four hundred Latin and three hundred German copies survive today.

Wondrous Punches and Types

Wood-block manuscripts were the first step toward mass-produced books. However, even before *The Nuremberg Chronicle* was published, a milestone in graphic arts was achieved with the invention of movable metal type. Although many people worked on various aspects of this type of printing, the credit for its invention goes to Johannes Gutenberg, who built the first printing press in Mainz, Germany, around 1450. This machine allowed printers to produce several books a day. Its importance is discussed by English author Stephen Fry: "The printing press was the world's first mass-production machine. Its invention . . . changed the world as dramatically as splitting the atom or sending men into space, sparking a cultural revolution that shaped the modern age. It is the machine that made us who we are today."[11]

Although it was used for mass production, book printing was considered an art form, humorously referred to as the black arts because printers were covered with ink. The first book to be produced through the black arts was the famous Gutenberg Bible. Each page of the Bible contains forty-two lines, and the entire book required over one hundred thousand pieces of cast type. By the time the Bible was printed, Gutenberg was so far in debt that his press belonged to his business partners, who published the book.

The two-volume Gutenberg Bible sold for three hundred florins, equal to three years' salary for an average clerk. However, this was considerably less than a handmade Bible, which could take a single monk twenty years to produce.

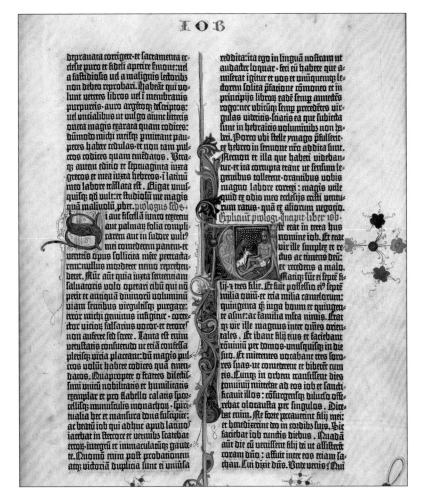

A page from the Gutenberg Bible. This was the first text to be printed using Johannes Gutenberg's printing press.

The next major project to come from Gutenberg's press was a Latin encyclopedia called the *Mainz Catholicon*. This work, written by religious scholar Johann Balbus in the thirteenth century, was a long instruction manual detailing religious practices. A printer's note at the back proudly boasts of the method of its creation: "With the help of the Most High at whose will the tongues of infants become eloquent . . . this noble book *Catholicon* has been printed and accomplished without the help of reed, stylus, or pen but by the wondrous agreement, proportion and harmony of [letter] punches and types."[12]

The creation of moveable type was revolutionary. Each printing press required the skills of only three workers, and these printers could produce about one hundred books a month. Within ten years typesetting technology had spread across Europe, and by 1500 there were thousands of printers in over two hundred cities in England, France, Italy, and the Netherlands. These printers engaged in a new field called job printing—producing pamphlets, calendars, religious writs, posters, and even playing cards. Some of this work was truly artistic, with printers using complicated four-color printing techniques devised by graphic designers who determined page layouts, typestyles, and ink colors.

The Art and Science of Letters

Like the Internet today, the printing press was a new technology that changed society. It came along during the Renaissance, when writers and artists were incorporating classical Greek philosophy and concepts of art into their work. In the field of graphics, designers turned their attention to the creation of different and distinctive sets of letters, numbers, and punctuation marks called typefaces. During this era, the flowery Gothic typeface used by scribes—and reproduced by Gutenberg—was replaced with a simplified Roman typeface similar to that used in ancient writing. In France, where King Francis I ordered all works to be printed in the Roman type, a designer named Geofroy Tory created an instruction manual codifying letter shapes, spelling rules, and the use of accents, quotation marks, and the apostrophe.

GUTENBERG'S PRESS

Johannes Gutenberg was a jeweler who understood processes involving carving and metal casting. When he invented the printing press, the major innovation was the method he devised for casting letters, or type.

Gutenberg made what is called a punch from steel that contained the mirror image of a letter. The punch was hammered into copper, a softer metal, to make a mold that was filled with a melted mixture of lead, tin, and antimony. This alloy was specially formulated by Gutenberg to melt easily and harden quickly.

The resulting cast pieces of type could be put together to form words, sentences, and paragraphs when fit into a rack. To print the page, the type in the rack was coated with a special ink made from linseed oil and soot, developed to adhere to the metal. Paper was laid on the inked type, and the rack was rolled into the printing press, which resembled a grape press with a wood screw. The screw was turned to lower a plate, or platen, in a firm, even pressure so the images of the letters were transferred onto the paper.

The title of Tory's book, *Champ Fleury*, is a French term that translates as the "flowery field of paradise." This expressive title was a result of the author's philosophy that states the shapes of letters should be based on the proportions of the human body. This is explained in the book's subtitle: *The Art and Science of the Proportion of . . . Ancient Roman Letters, According to the Human Body and Face.*

Tory was a scholar, editor, scribe, illuminator, and bookseller. To lay out perfectly proportioned letters, he designed a square grid that foreshadowed the method used for type design in the twentieth century. (It is also the basis for the pixels of computerized letterforms.) Tory's detailed letters had to be reproduced with refined printing methods, so his books were published with a process called intaglio, Italian for "to incise." Intaglio allows graphic artists to cut, or engrave, illustrations into copper plates that are used for printing.

Although it is an ancient technique, intaglio did not come into use in Europe until the fifteenth century. Another intaglio process, mezzotint, or "half tint," allowed artists to create a rich range of gray tones between black and white and was ideal for printing portraits. To create a mezzotint, the artist uses a metal tool with small teeth that roughs up the plate with thousands of tiny dots that hold ink.

The intaglio process opened up yet another avenue for graphic artists, allowing just about any illustration to be printed.

Diderot's *Encyclopédie* used the intaglio process to produce its illustrations.

This set the stage for a wave of publishing that included scientific and medical illustrations as well as books of art and music. However, the process could not be used on the same page as type, so books had illustrations on one page with the text on the opposite page.

The intaglio process reached its apex with the publication of Denis Diderot's *Encyclopédie* in the early 1770s. The seventeen volumes of printed text were accompanied by eleven volumes of illustrations, or plates. Diderot believed "a glance at an object or its representation is more informative than a page of text."[13]

Nymphic, Mystic, and Glyphic

Beginning in the early nineteenth century, there was a proliferation of type design led by printer and typographer (typeface designer) Firmin Didot. His type, called Didot, was valued for its contrasting thick and thin strokes. Didot also used hairline serifs, short decorative strokes added to letters.

Many typefaces, or fonts, were developed based on Didot's designs and remain in use today. In Italy engraver, printer, and typographer Giambattista Bodoni developed the famous font that bares his name. Bodoni is similar to Didot but with smaller serifs. Today Didoni, a font that joins both their typefaces, also combines the two typographers' names.

In England the Figgins Foundry took advantage of the fad for Egyptian art and artifacts, creating the Egyptian font, a typeface called slab faced because of its thick, fat, broad letters that are augmented with large, square serifs. Other slab-faced types followed, including Latin and Clarendon. Together these new typefaces changed the visual design of books, posters, and other graphic material.

By the mid-1800s type foundries were competing to invent the most decorative fonts to catch the consumer's eye. In the United States, the Shniedenwend and Lee Foundry developed typefaces with fantastic names such as Nymphic, Mystic, Glyphic, Aesthetic, and Attic. These fonts, which can be found on the Internet, represented creative advances in print arts. However, the most prolific typefaces came from the drafting

Frederic Goudy designed 124 different fonts over the course of his career.

board of Frederic Goudy, an American book designer, author, and printer. Goudy designed Camelot, his first typeface, in 1896. In later years he created Oldstyle, Kennerly, Garamond, Deepdone, and Forum. His most well-known font, Goudy, is popular for its elegant design and readability. In all, Goudy created 124 fonts, not only drawing them, but casting them in his foundry.

Beyond Gutenberg

The number of new fonts coincided with a growing demand for books throughout the nineteenth century. And nearly every aspect of book production in Europe and the United States was changing rapidly due to the Industrial Revolution. It was an era of factories, automation, and mass production driven by the invention of the steam engine. Around 1820 Gutenberg's old-style, hand-operated wooden press was replaced by steam-powered presses that allowed press operators to produce over one thousand pages per hour. In the 1830s the invention of automatic type casters allowed a worker to fabricate up to twenty thousand pieces of type a day.

In the 1880s several inventions that appeared within a few years of each other once again revolutionized the book arts. In 1885 German inventor Ottmar Mergenthaler invented the linotype machine. Since Gutenberg's day, printers had been

A woman working on a linotype machine in a publishing house.

using hundreds of individual letters to form sentences and paragraphs. The linotype, which could be operated by one person, fused the letters into a long, solid line, or slug, of molten lead. The slugs could later be melted down and the lead reused to make more type.

In 1886 the book arts were revolutionized once again when Frederick Ives invented the halftone printing process. This allowed printers to reproduce photographs as a series of black-and-white dots with full ranges of gray. Before this method was developed, photographic prints had to be pasted onto individual pages of books, an awkward and expensive process. With the introduction of halftones, books with photographs of exotic locations, war zones, and scientific subjects were instant best sellers, and publishers could barely keep up with public demand.

New Typography

New technology changed the look of books. But as printers focused on mass production, the quality of graphic design suffered as pages were muddied with long, dense lines of type and small margins. This began to change in the 1920s with the advent of the new typography movement in Germany. Calligrapher and printer Jan Tschichold, one of the leading voices of new typography, sought to formalize rules of book design that emphasized clarity, arrangement, and readability.

Tschichold believed that typographers should abandon the lavish, serif fonts of the so-called old typography movement and adopt type without serifs, or sans serif. In October 1925 he summarized his views in the manifesto "Elementary Typography" in the German trade magazine *Typographic News*:

> The new typography emphasizes function. The goal of every typography is communication. . . . Communication must appear in the shortest, simplest and most forceful form. . . . The basic typeface form is the sans serif typeface in all variations: light, semibold, bold, condensed to extended. Typefaces that . . . are not elementally designed . . . limit the possibility of international understanding.[14]

THE NEW TYPOGRAPHY

In 1928 German calligrapher and graphic designer Jan Tschichold published The New Typography, *featuring contemporary rules for book design. The book challenged long-held traditions and was considered so radical it was banned by the Nazis in 1932. Below, graphic artist Roy Johnson explores the contents of* The New Typography:

Tschichold looks at typography in a historical context, then explores the developments in twentieth century art. . . . The principles of the new typography are then explained as a revolutionary movement towards clarity and readability; a rejection of superfluous [unnecessary] decoration; and an insistence on the primacy of functionality in design. There are chapters on the use of photographs; the standardisation of paper sizes . . . lots of carefully analysed examples of business stationery, and even film posters. . . . All this is illustrated by some crisp and still attractive reproductions of everyday graphics—letterheads, postcards, catalogues, and posters—in the red, black and white colour-scheme characteristic of the period.

Roy Johnson, *The New Typography*, Mantex. www.mantex.co.uk/reviews/tsch-01.htm.

While these words may sound rather mundane, they created controversy in the graphic arts community while making Tschichold famous. Many typesetters were at first reluctant to abandon the old typestyles, but within a few years ornamental fonts disappeared from books.

Tschichold also believed that books were difficult to read when each line was centered on the page. While this symmetry had long been viewed by old typographers as beautiful and harmonious, Tschichold advocated asymmetry. He thought that sentences should be flush left, that is, aligned on the left but of various lengths on the right. This design was meant to attract and hold the viewer's attention. Tschichold believed this was necessary because readers faced a deluge of mailings, magazines, and newspapers every day. Rather than reading each line, they glanced at material and only decided to read it if it appeared interesting. With asymmetric columns on a page, Tschichold believed publishers could stimulate that interest.

Penguin Rules

Today nearly every publication uses flush left typography. But Tschichold's ideas were considered so radical in 1932 that when Adolf Hitler came to power the Nazis seized all of Tschichold's writings, saying they were threatening the well-being of the German people. The calligrapher fled to England, where he went to work in 1947 as a designer for Penguin Books.

The founder of Penguin, Allen Lane, wanted to make quality literature available to the public for the same price as a pack of cigarettes. In order to reach the widest market, Penguin sold its books in general stores and subway stations rather than bookstores. This concept revolutionized graphic arts once again, because the book covers featured bright colors coded for book content, which was meant to attract maximum interest among other products sold in stores. Orange and white covers meant the book was general fiction, green and white was crime fiction, and red and white was travel and adventure.

Tschichold developed the Penguin Composition Rules to standardize the look of the books. The rules covered text composition, indenting paragraphs, punctuation, the use of capitals and italics, and rules for footnotes and references.

Tschichold remained a guiding force in book design. His trade magazine essays, written between 1937 and his death in 1974, were compiled in 1991 in *The Form of the Book*. Within those pages the graphic artist instructs readers on every aspect of book design. Topics include the size and shape of pages, cover and title page design, paper color, typefaces, margins, paragraphs, section headings, footnotes, indexes, colophons, and even the blank pages before a book's back cover.

Penguin paperback books from the 1930s. Penguin Books set out to make books that would be available cheaply to consumers and would visually attract their attention.

While advances in technology changed the methods used to produce books over the years, Tschichold's rules remain popular and are widely used today. They are used by graphic artists designing books, glossy magazines, newspapers, and Web sites.

Because of design traditions that can be traced back to monks in their scriptoria, books are more than just a jumble of inky words on paper. They are pleasing to the eyes, comfortable to hold, and can provide countless hours of enjoyment.

The Art of
the Poster

Anyone traveling through a modern city is inundated with graphic design images. Mobile posters advertise products on the sides of buses and taxis, while giant billboards loom above streets. Posters hang in store windows to entice shoppers, and fences and utility poles are covered with flyers hawking rock bands, public events, and political candidates. Such is the case from Iowa to Istanbul. The world would look like a different place without the poster.

Because posters are nearly everywhere, some consider them a form of visual pollution. But the roots of the modern poster can be traced to French artists in the second half of the nineteenth century. And the advertising posters they produced were so beloved that in 1885 art critic René Martin wrote in the leading Paris newspaper *Le Figaro*, "More talent goes into a poster than into many [paintings] that make a sensation."[15]

Grease, Water, and Ink

Like many advances in the graphic arts, the rise of the poster can be traced to the invention of a new technology. In this case it was lithography, Greek for "stone printing," discovered in

1798 by Alois Senefelder, an Austrian playwright. Senefelder was driven to his discovery by sheer necessity. Although he had written one successful play, he found he was too poor to pay a printer to publish his second play. In an effort to print the play himself, Senefelder experimented unsuccessfully with various methods, using etched stones and metal plates. One day as he was puzzling over his conundrum, his mother called out a long list of items she wanted him to pick up when he went out. Lacking a sheet of paper, Senefelder picked up a grease pencil and scribbled his mother's list on a flat printing stone he had nearby.

The writing element of Senefelder's grease pencil was made from oil-based wax and black pigment. After he used it on the stone he realized a basic scientific principle: oil and water do not mix. Eventually he devised the lithographic method. He drew an image on a stone with the grease pencil and then spread water over the entire stone, which moistened all the areas except the grease image, which repelled the water. An oil-based ink was rolled over the stone, but it only adhered to the image. A sheet of paper was placed over the illustration, a roller was applied, and the image was transferred to the paper.

Senefelder's lithography was the first new printing technology since Gutenberg's press. And he soon realized that by using three stones with three colors—blue, red, and yellow—he could print an infinite variety of blended colors. Commenting on the possibilities of three-color lithography in his 1819 book *The Invention of Lithography*, Senefelder wrote:

If this [process] is done just right, and if, of course, the drawing bears the impress of a masterly hand, and if the printer understands his art, the impression will be perfectly like an original drawing, so that the most skilled etcher in copper hardly can attain the same effect. Therefore this method, which has the further advantage of being a quick one, is excellently well adapted for copying paintings.[16]

Le Style Mucha

In the 1890s artist and illustrator Alphonse Mucha was one of the most famous graphic designers in the world, and the French referred to art nouveau as *Le Style Mucha*. According to the Alphonse Mucha Biography Web page, Mucha's style "was based on a strong composition, sensuous curves derived from nature, refined decorative elements and natural colors. The Art Nouveau precepts were used, too, but never at the expense of his vision."

Mucha's career took off in 1895 when he signed a six-year contract with Sarah Bernhardt to design all of the posters, sets, and costumes for her theatrical productions. Bernhardt was the most renowned actress in the world, and Mucha's association with her brought great success. In 1898 he illustrated the best-selling *Ilsee, Princess de Tripoli*, a fairy tale based on a Bernhardt play, and held a popular one-man show in Paris. Mucha also found a unique way to get his art into the marketplace. He published his graphics with Champenois, a printer that also promoted the work through postcards and *panneaux*—sets of four large images around a central theme such as four seasons, four times of day, and four flowers. These images were printed on silk and sold for high prices to collectors. In 1900 Mucha worked with a goldsmith to create jewelry based on his designs and also wrote a book, *Documents Decoratifs*, which contained his artistic theories. Although the book was meant for art students, it was primarily used by Mucha's imitators, who used the great designer's talents for their own benefit.

Jim Vadeboncoeur Jr., "Alphonse Mucha Biography," Been Publishing I'm Back. www.bpib.com/illustrat/mucha.htm.

The Father of the Modern Poster

Lithography allowed artists and illustrators, for the first time, to draw their designs directly onto the printing surface. This meant those unfamiliar with intaglio could reproduce detailed designs, as Senefelder said, quickly and easily. By the 1840s further advances in the lithographic process allowed designers to print amazingly realistic imagery. This was used to publish graphics of every description, including maps, portraits, historical scenes, product labels, and even Christmas cards. Elaborate designs could use up to forty different stones to achieve intricate, layered imagery.

The most competitive field in lithography was in the printing of pictorial advertisement posters called signboards. These could be produced at the rate of ten thousand sheets per hour. And lithographers could make large posters about 32 by 46 inches (81 by 117 cm), whereas the average printing press could only produce work 10 by 15 inches (25 by 38 cm) in size.

In this era before movies and television, people sought entertainment at carnivals, circuses, expositions, concerts, and plays. There was fierce competition for the public's money, and posters were the bait that promoters used to attract customers. In this competitive environment, printing firms hired the leading artists and illustrators of the day to create attractive, eye-catching posters. At the Paris printing firm Rouchon, muralist Paul Baudry produced posters with bright, oddly clashing colors that were difficult to ignore. Another Parisian painter and lithographer, Jules Chéret, went beyond the crass commercialism and established lithography as the leading creative medium of the day. He is now known as the father of the modern poster.

Les Chérettes

Chéret's career began in 1849 when he was thirteen and his father bought him a three-year apprenticeship in a Paris lithography shop. After studying art and lithography in France and Britain, he established a Paris lithography firm in 1866. When he printed a large theatrical poster for a production featuring world-famous actress Sarah Bernhardt, it was the first visual poster of its type.

In 1881 Chéret sold his firm but remained the company's art director. This allowed him to spend his days designing and drawing his illustrations on lithographic stones. He perfected a technique to print his work in sections, which allowed his printers to produce posters that were 7 feet (2m) high. The press run on a single such poster might be as many as two hundred thousand copies in a year.

Chéret's graphic designs featured a bright range of attention-grabbing colors with details filled in with stipples (dot patterns) and crosshatching (short intersecting lines). Rather than use lines of standard type, he often drew his letters freehand, arching the words around central figures or splashing letters across the page.

A poster by Jules Chéret, featuring a Chéret girl. Chéret is considered the father of the modern poster.

Chéret's design innovations were responsible for major changes in French culture and fashion in an era known as *la belle époque*, or the beautiful era, a term used to describe the fabulous nightlife of Paris. Chéret's posters featured scantily clad dancers kicking up their heels, peering over their shoulders, spinning, and flying through the air. The high-stepping models were laughing and effervescent, symbols of the carefree Paris nightlife. When the posters appeared by the thousands on the walls of Paris, young women imitated the looks of the Chéret girls, or *Les Chérettes*. In *A History of Graphic Design*, educator and designer Philip B. Meggs explains how Chéret's graphic art transformed French society:

> The beautiful young women he created, dubbed "Chérettes" by an admiring public, were archetypes [classic examples]—not only for the idealized presentation of women in mass media but for a generation of French women who used [the models'] dress and apparent lifestyle as inspiration. One pundit dubbed Chéret "the father of women's liberation" because his women introduced a new role model in the late Victorian era. Options for women were limited, and the proper lady in the drawing room and the trollop in the bordello were stereotyped roles, when into this dichotomy swept the Chérette. Neither prudes nor prostitutes, these self-assured, happy women enjoyed life to the fullest, wearing low-cut dresses, dancing, drinking wine, and even smoking in public.[17]

Because of his work, Chéret was awarded the highest decoration a Frenchman can receive. Meggs writes that Chéret was named to the Legion of Honor for "creating a new branch of art that advanced printing and served the needs of commerce and industry."[18] There was only one problem with the public's love of his work: The posters were often stolen off the walls as quickly as they were put up. However, Chéret created over one thousand designs, and with massive print runs, some of the originals are still available for purchase today.

A "Sadness That Breathes"

Chéret's girls may have represented a new type of woman in France, but the designer's main competition in the 1890s was no stranger to prostitutes and dancing girls. And the posters designed by French painter and illustrator Henri de Toulouse-Lautrec captured scenes in Paris cabarets, or pleasure palaces, in an entirely different manner.

Lautrec was a well-known figure at the Moulin Rouge, known as "the largest market-place for love in Paris."[19] And the artist's 1891 poster *La Goulue, Moulin Rouge* is an icon of late-nineteenth-century graphic art. On this large poster, 67 by 48 inches (170 by 122 cm), Lautrec seemed deliberately to contradict the joyful images of Chéret. Rather than portray an intricately drawn fantasy girl, Lautrec depicted an actual cancan dancer with large fields of color and few details.

The dress of the dancer, named La Goulue, is a blob of white. The foot of her stocking-clad leg disappears behind the head of a male dancer, known as Valentine, who is placed in the foreground. Although he is wearing a tall top hat, Valentine does not appear as an elegant, fashionable dancer, but a rather a rumpled, almost solitary figure. In the background a faceless crowd stands in black silhouette with the profile of Lautrec himself on one side.

As a regular patron of dance-hall prostitutes, Lautrec understood the dancer's isolation amidst the jolly ribaldry of the Paris "love market." And through his graphic skills, he was able to portray the loneliness to a viewer at a glance. This message was not lost on French illustrator and artist Ernest Maindron, who wrote that he was "struck by the sadness that breathes from [Lautrec's] work."[20]

Organic, Plantlike Lines

Unlike the prolific Chéret, Lautrec's poster production was limited to only thirty-two. This succeeded in making his limited illustrations more attractive to art collectors and helped spawn what was called poster mania in the 1890s. But Lautrec's

Henri de Toulouse-Lautrec's poster *La Goulue, Moulin Rouge* became an icon of late-nineteenth-century graphic art.

influence went beyond the commercial market of art buyers and sellers. His use of radically flat figures, silhouettes, symbolic shapes, and expressive imagery inspired a generation of poster artists. And the streets of Paris served as their art gallery.

The poster fad coincided with the art nouveau (new art) movement that was also gripping France. This highly decorative style was characterized by flowing, curved lines and ornamental flower or plant patterns. Meggs provides a description of the style:

> Art Nouveau's identifying visual quality is an organic, plantlike line. Freed from roots and gravity, [the line] can either undulate with whiplash energy or flow with elegant grace as it defines, modulates, and decorates a given space. Vine tendrils, flowers (such as the rose and lily), birds (particularly peacocks), and the human female form were frequent motifs [reoccurring themes] from which this fluid line was adapted.[21]

Art nouveau, a style based on the British arts and crafts movement, was popular in France between 1890 and 1910. Proponents of the movement attempted to remove the dividing line between art and audience, believing that everything should be art. To make their point, they put the art nouveau style on wallpaper, Paris metro stations, dishes, clothing, light fixtures, doorways, and stained glass.

"Gismonda"

In the world of graphics, art nouveau's key proponent was Czech artist Alphonse Mucha. In fact, because of the popularity of his posters, Parisians referred to art nouveau as *Le Style Mucha*. However, Mucha rejected the art nouveau label, believing art was ancient, eternal, and never new.

Mucha became famous virtually overnight in late 1894, mainly as an accident of fate. The illustrator was laboring in a Paris lithography shop on Christmas Eve when an emergency arose. Sarah Bernhardt was unhappy with the poster Mucha's employer had created for her new production, *Gismonda*. She demanded a new one to be ready on opening day on New Year's Eve. Since Mucha was the only available artist working the night before Christmas, the shop owner gave him the commission. The illustrator rose to the occasion and created a poster so thoroughly different that it became an instant collector's item.

Alphonse Mucha's radical design for the *Gismonda* poster made him famous overnight.

In a five-color lithograph that epitomized the art nouveau style, the beloved actress is depicted life-size as the central female figure in the design. Her head is crowned with pink flowers, and her flowing gown and scarf feature motifs of vines, plants, and animals.

As a result of *Gismonda,* Mucha was catapulted to fame. He immediately signed a six-year contract with Bernhardt, going on to produce nine exceptional posters for her. He also designed stage sets, costumes, publicity, and jewelry for Bernhardt's many productions.

War and Propaganda

Art nouveau crossed the ocean to the United States around 1900 and was prominently featured on the covers of *Harper's* and other magazines. However, poster mania had run its course in France, and Mucha and other illustrators such as Eugène Grasset and Emmanuel Orazi moved on to other projects.

By the 1910s *la belle époque* also faded into history, replaced by a modern era of electric lights, airplanes, automobiles, and heavy machinery. And in many cases, the lithographic process was replaced by the updated printing press, which could reproduce posters faster, cheaper, and in greater quantity.

The growing industrialization of Europe also allowed nations to build new,

THE MANY FACES OF UNCLE SAM

The poster of Uncle Sam pointing his finger and saying "I Want You for U.S. Army" is a classic image that achieved iconic status in the twentieth century. Like many well-known works of art, James Montgomery Flagg's illustration has been parodied countless times over the years. During the Vietnam War era, a group of antiwar graphic designers formed the Committee to Help Unsell the War. Their 1971 contribution showed a bruised and bloodied Uncle Sam reaching out his hand with the caption "I Want Out."

In more recent times, artist Stephen Kroninger protested the Gulf War of 1991 by showing President George H.W. Bush as Uncle Sam. The typography in the poster consisted of cut out letters resembling a kidnapper's ransom note. The caption read "Uncle George Wants You to Forget Failing Banks, Education, Drugs, AIDS, Poor Health Care, Unemployment, Crime, Racism, Corruption, and Have a Good War."

Eleven years later, the Web site TomPaine.com ran a parody meant to protest the Iraq War. Uncle Sam was replaced on the recruiting poster with terrorist mastermind Osama bin Laden, or Uncle oSAMa. Indicating that the war in Iraq would help Bin Laden recruit more terrorists, Osama points his finger and says "I Want You to Invade Iraq."

Other parodies include messages such as "I Want You to End the Ban on Gays in the Military," "I Want Your Oil!" and the computer-related "I Want You to Help Fight Spam." Whatever the cause, the Uncle Sam graphic design proves that a classic image can be timeless and used to communicate many different ideas over the years.

deadly machines of war. This led to tragic results in 1914 when World War I broke out, with Germany and Austria on one side and France and Great Britain on the other.

During the war, which eventually involved the United States and Canada as well as numerous European nations, governments had to achieve several goals. They needed to recruit soldiers, raise money to finance the war, and convince people to conserve, plant vegetable gardens, and recycle in order to prevent shortages of important resources. In addition, governments created propaganda to vilify the enemy, publicize atrocities committed by the enemy, and declare that the enemy threatened civilization. In this era before radio or television, the task of communicating these objectives to the public fell to poster artists.

At the outbreak of the war, Germany was a world leader in printing technology and graphic design, so it is not surprising that they were the first to produce propaganda posters. Their style was based on the *sachplakat*, or object poster, invented in Germany in 1906 by graphic designer Lucian Bernhard. The object poster reduces design elements to a minimum, featuring a product in flat colors, a logo with solid shadows, and a line or two of bold type usually in hand-drawn block letters.

Bernhard originally designed the *sachplakat* to stand out among the art nouveau posters that were plastered on nearly every wall and fence in Berlin. However, when he used these design techniques on a poster for a 1915 war loan campaign, the results must surely have frightened Germany's enemies. Reprinted in international graphics magazines, the poster features the clinched fist of a medieval knight, wearing armored gloves that resemble brass knuckles. The lettering, in the ancient Gothic Franktur typeface, says, "This [fist] is the way to peace—the enemy wills it so! Thus subscribe to the war loan!"[22]

Strong Designs, Simple Messages

The Americans and British took a different approach to wartime posters, relying on vivid painted illustrations rather than stark graphics. But the goal was the same—to inspire fear and hatred of the enemy. A poster designed by respected illustrator Joseph Pinnell for the Fourth Liberty Loan bond drive in 1918 was typical of the era. It shows the Statue of Liberty surrounded by bright orange flames and New York City, in the background, engulfed in flames. Overhead, German airplanes fly through the sky dropping bombs. Beneath this menacing picture, a gold box with black capital letters states: "THAT LIBERTY SHALL NOT PERISH FROM THE EARTH BUY LIBERTY BONDS."[23]

Pinnell's poster was one of the most popular of the war, and the illustrator emphasized the importance of graphic arts during wartime: "When the United States wished to make public its wants, whether of men or money, it found that art—as the European countries had found—was the best medium."[24]

The famous World War I recruitment poster "I Want You for U.S. Army" used a strong design and simple message to attract attention.

By far the most recognizable image from the era is the military recruitment poster *I Want You for U.S. Army*, showing Uncle Sam, with his white goatee and top hat, pointing a long index finger at the viewer. Five million copies were printed of this poster designed by graphic artist James Montgomery Flagg, and it is one of the most recognizable graphic images of the twentieth century. It was among the first of many posters directly addressing the viewer, and as art curator Therese Heyman writes, "Flagg's popular poster demonstrates the commanding effectiveness of a strong design and simple message."[25]

We Can Do It!

In the mid-1930s, as the threat of World War II was growing, the poster was once again drafted into the service of conquest. In Germany, the Nazis were masters of propaganda, and their leader, Adolf Hitler, consciously created fear-provoking symbols to represent his regime graphically. These included the right-facing German imperial eagle and the black swastika on a field of red and white. However, after the war began in 1939, German cities were under aerial bombardment, which disrupted the ability of the Nazis to produce propaganda.

In the United States, the power of the poster was well understood during World War II. In the early days of fighting, the government set up a special unit, the Office of Wartime Information, to employ graphic designers, illustrators, and artists for the cause. These people created posters that were placed in libraries, post offices, schools, factories, and other public places. The World War II Poster Collection from the Northwestern University Library Web site explains the many important themes featured in posters of World War II:

> Some address home efforts for conservation of materials and rationing; others exhort workers to greater productivity and quality output; while others warn of the dangers of innocently leaking critical defense information to unsuspecting enemy agents. Women are encouraged to work in factories or military support positions, and

This poster featuring Rosie the Riveter revised the feminine ideal to emphasize strength and courage in a time of war.

instructed how to behave in these situations. Some of the posters are targeted directly at school children, including charts illustrating how specific savings amounts could outfit the equipment and supplies needed by a brave G.I. soldier. Various [poster] series address themes such as nutrition or investment in war bonds.[26]

The posters that urged women to work had patriotic themes, showing secretaries behind their typewriters saluting the viewer. Others played on the emotional aspect of the conflict, such as Lawrence Wilbur's illustration of a distressed woman above the caption "Longing Won't Bring Him Back Sooner . . . Get a War Job!"[27] However, one of the most enduring images from this era highlighted the strengths of women. J. Howard Miller's *We Can Do It!* features Rosie the Riveter, a woman dressed in overalls and bandanna, flexing the muscles of her right arm. As the National Archives explains, the image in the poster was meant to change long entrenched societal ideas about women: "[Rosie] was introduced as a symbol of patriotic womanhood. The accoutrements of war work—uniforms, tools, and lunch pails—were incorporated [to revise the] image of the feminine ideal."[28]

Going "Graphically Crazy"

After the war ended, most women stopped working as millions of returning soldiers replaced them in the factories and offices. The poster as a tool of social change and propaganda was forgotten for two decades, until another sort of revolution erupted.

In the mid-1960s thousands of young adults in San Francisco began experimenting with LSD and other psychedelic drugs after attending parties called "acid tests." These events were organized by the Merry Pranksters, a group of rebels led by Ken Kesey, best-selling author of *One Flew over the Cuckoo's Nest*. LSD was legal at the time, and the events were publicized with posters unlike any ever seen before. Norman Hartweg's *Can You Pass the Acid Test?* poster advertised the parties and entertainment such as the Grateful Dead, the Fugs, and poet Allen Ginsburg. Every space on the poster is filled with random images, such as comic book figures, and silly, nonsensical comments. The free-form, flowing lettering on the posters is shaded with stripes, checks, spots, paisley

Wes Wilson claimed that his poster designs, such as this concert poster for the rock band The Grateful Dead, were inspired by his experiences with LSD.

patterns, and American flags. While this hand-drawn poster is raw and amateurish, it set the stage for the poster revolution that was to follow.

The acid tests ended in October 1966 when LSD was outlawed. However, a handful of largely unschooled artists who had attended the acid tests remade the world of visual design. Alton Kelly, Stanley Mouse, Victor Moscoso, Robert "Wes" Wilson, and Rick Griffin began designing posters for rock concerts and covers for record albums. They used swirling lines, Victorian imagery, Native American designs, and art nouveau fonts.

Wilson said he used colors and patterns taken from his visual experiences with LSD. Moscoso used sharply contrasting lines that created optical illusions such as afterimages on the retina and other distortions similar to a drug experience. Mouse and Kelly, who worked together, spent hours in the San Francisco library paging through old books from the 1800s, taking imagery from American Indian photographs. One of their most famous images, the skull with a crown of red roses made for the Grateful Dead, first appeared on the 1971 album *Skull and Roses*. This image, which was associated with the Grateful Dead for the next twenty-five years, was adapted from an illustration in a nineteenth-century publication of *The Rubaiyat of Omar Khayyam*. Before his death in 2008, Kelly told the *San Francisco Chronicle*:

> Stanley and I had no idea what we were doing. But we went ahead and looked at American Indian stuff, Chinese stuff, Art Nouveau, Art Deco, Modern . . . whatever. We were stunned by what we found and what we were able to do. We had free rein to just go graphically crazy. Where before that, all advertising was pretty much just typeset with a photograph of something.[29]

Rather than use set type around this medley of wild imagery, the poster artists went out of their way to make the words nearly impossible to understand. As Meggs writes, "According to newspaper reports, respectable and intelligent businessmen were unable to comprehend the lettering on the posters, yet they communicated well enough to fill auditoriums with a younger generation who deciphered, rather than read, the message."[30]

By the late 1960s graphics like those on San Francisco's psychedelic posters had spread across American consumer culture. Similar images were seen on buttons, bumper stickers, clothing, cars, countless record albums, and even ads in

Milton Glaser's poster for *Bob Dylan's Greatest Hits* featured Dylan's hair in wild colors.

THE PEACE SYMBOL

In the mid-1960s graphic art exploded off the printed page, where it had been for a thousand years, and onto buttons, bumper stickers, and T-shirts. One of the most ubiquitous examples of this graphic arts revolution was the peace symbol.

The forked symbol representing peace was actually a product of the 1950s. It was designed by British graphic arts professional Gerald Holtom for a 1958 London peace march organized by the Direct Action Committee Against Nuclear War and the Campaign for Nuclear Disarmament. Holtom had convinced the groups that their message would have a greater impact if they had a simple visual image, and the peace symbol was born. The designer used two letters from the semaphore, or military flag-signaling, alphabet. He overlaid the symbol for the letter *N* (nuclear) over the letter *D* (disarmament). Holtom placed the letters in a circle that represented Earth.

The peace symbol was imported into the United States by Philip Altbach, a member of the Student Peace Union (SPU), a college antiwar group formed in the late 1950s. The SPU sold thousands of peace symbol buttons on college campuses. By 1967, when the anti–Vietnam War movement was growing rapidly, the peace symbol seemed to be everywhere. The graphic symbol of peace remains popular among antiwar protesters today.

The peace symbol was created from the semaphore symbols for N (for nuclear) and D (for disarmament) inside a circle that symbolized Earth.

mainstream media. Meanwhile, in New York, designer Milton Glaser was putting his own spin on the counterculture graphics revolt at his Push Pin Studio.

Push Pin's style went beyond the psychedelic, combining aspects of the arts and crafts, art nouveau, and art deco movements with contemporary typography and illustration. Glaser designed one of the most iconic images from the 1960s, the incredibly popular poster for the 1967 album *Bob Dylan's Greatest Hits*. The poster features a silhouette of Bob Dylan's face and head in black while portraying his wildly dramatic hair in exotic, electric colors.

Punk Attitude

Graphic styles inspired by the 1960s are still popular, especially in the world of fashion. Skate and surf-wear companies such as Quicksilver and Fallen produce shoes, shirts, dresses, and skateboards with designs that would have been coveted in the 1960s.

Although surf graphics have been modernized with a punk attitude, the free-form designs have roots in illustrations by San Francisco artists who, in turn, were influenced by Chéret and Mucha. Whatever their origins, the posters communicate messages to the masses, combining letters and pictures into graphic images that have become timeless.

Designing for the Masses

The word *magazine* comes from the Arabic *makhazin*, which means "storehouse" or "warehouse." And there is little doubt that the pages of general interest magazines are storehouses for the best a culture has to offer. Magazines have long published the words from society's greatest novelists, journalists, and essayists. Writings of authors such as Edgar Allan Poe, Kurt Vonnegut, Joyce Carol Oates, and Toni Morrison have all appeared on the pages of magazines. So has the work of the greatest artists, including Pablo Picasso, Salvador Dali, and Jackson Pollock, as well as classic photographs by Ansel Adams, Margaret Bourke-White, Richard Avedon, and Annie Leibovitz.

Magazines also act as warehouses for the worst society has to offer, including sleazy gossip, rumors, propaganda, and bloody images of war and hatred. And between the best and the worst are the advertisements, which finance most magazines. Without ads, publishers could not pay artists, writers, photographers, and graphic designers to fill their pages. And, like the magazines, advertisements have been the driving forces behind graphic design innovations. Some of the greatest artists, writers, and photographers are paid to create them.

"When It Rains It Pours"

The modern magazine can trace its roots back to the mid-nineteenth century, when a convergence of events provided a ripe environment for growth. By this time the Industrial Revolution had been churning out consumer goods for a generation. Where there had once been a lack of mass-produced clothes, canned food, health remedies, and tools there was now a glut of these products. This created an intense competition among manufacturers. Companies that never had to advertise before were now forced to use brash sales techniques to reach consumers. This resulted in Volney Palmer founding the first business known as an advertising agency in Philadelphia in 1843.

Palmer was an ad broker—he bought ad space for companies in newspapers. N.W. Ayer opened the world's first full-service ad agency in Philadelphia in 1869. Ayer had a creative staff for planning and executing ad campaigns. Professional art editors hired illustrators to supervise the layouts of ads. The completed ads were then turned over to workers who specialized in ad placement in various publications.

The Ayer ad agency operated successfully until 2002. It is widely known for its famous advertising slogans, including "When it rains it pours" for Morton Salt (1912), "I'd walk a mile for a Camel" for R.J. Reynolds Tobacco (1921), and "A diamond is forever" for De Beers (1948).

"The Whole Periodical Was Changed"

Advertising agencies needed to reach the widest audience with their campaigns, and by 1880 there were over twenty-six hundred different magazines in the United States alone. While there was a high failure rate for magazines, several became national icons in the first decades of the twentieth century, including *Vogue*, *Vanity Fair*, *Harper's Weekly*, *House and Garden*, *Ladies' Home Journal*, and *The Saturday Evening Post*. These and other magazines attracted astounding sums of money from advertisers. For example, in 1909 magazine publishers collectively

Before the advent of television and the Internet, magazines played a major role in shaping society and culture. From the all-important cover image to the ad on the last page and all the ads and articles in between, the magazine influenced public opinion, promoted shared ideals, and helped people understand the world around them.

From the 1890s through the 1960s, when magazines experienced their greatest popularity, cover illustrations had the power to produce national icons. For example, the Gibson Girl created one of the earliest national standards for feminine beauty in the United States. These illustrations of full-figured women with wasp-thin waists, created by Charles Dana Gibson, first appeared on the cover of *Life* in the 1890s. This set off a twenty-year fad for Gibson Girls that saw the romanticized images appearing on dishes, ashtrays, pillow covers, fans, and tablecloths as well as magazine covers.

Norman Rockwell was another enormously influential illustrator. His idealized pictures of daily life in America appeared on the covers of *The Saturday Evening Post* magazine for more than fifty years. According to graphic designers Steven Heller and Louise Fili in *Cover Story*, Rockwell's covers "offered a vision of the United States as mythic as any religious tableau."

Beyond their cultural influence, magazines long served as showcases for the most fashionable artistic concepts and trends in graphic design. Whether it

was art nouveau in the 1890s, art deco in the 1920s, or modernism in postwar years, these styles of visual communication reached their widest audience in magazine layouts and advertisements.

Steven Heller and Louise Fili, *Cover Story*. San Francisco: Chronicle, 1996, p. 8.

Norman Rockwell's illustrations, such as this one for The Saturday Evening Post, *featured an idealized vision of daily American life.*

earned over $202 million from advertising, the equivalent of $4.6 billion in 2008. By 1919 that number had doubled.

Ad agencies clamored to place larger ads than their competitors in the most popular magazines. This forced the periodicals to hire their own ad managers and art directors to make sense from the chaos. A good example is *Ladies' Home Journal*, where the pages were a jumble of opposing ads until graphic designer John Adams Thayer was hired in 1892 to clean up the visuals. According to the magazine's typographer, Frank Presby:

> Thayer made up a set of rules for the *Ladies' Home Journal* advertising columns that changed them from the ugly black mess produced by the desire of advertisers to outdo all others and gave them instead an appearance pleasing to the eye. Illustration was likewise censored into a more artistic appearance. The aspect of the whole periodical was changed.[31]

Dramatic Images

The techniques pioneered by Thayer gave rise to new, sophisticated standards of graphic representation. His work was aided by advances in halftone printing technology, which led magazines to switch from muddy, engraved illustrations to crisp, clean photographs. Journalism professors Sammye Johnson and Patricia Prijatel explain the benefits of photography, or halftones, in graphic design:

> More and more magazines began using halftones to embellish articles. *McClure's*, for example, included photographs from the lives of famous men in its "Human Document" series, while *Munsey's* used the nude female to illustrate a department titled "Artists and Their Work." Photos were still black and white, yet the images were nonetheless dramatic. *Collier's* news photographs of the 1898 Spanish-American War established the publication as the premier picture magazine of the time.[32]

This cover of the August 1908 edition of *The Ladies' Home Journal* shows the type of color illustrations made possible by process color.

The change to photos saved publishers great sums of money. A halftone reproduction cost about twenty dollars, whereas the price of an engraved illustration was about three hundred dollars. And the halftone process also allowed publishers to print in full color without the time and expense of lithography.

Because color photo film was not yet invented, color illustrations were shot as halftones. In what is known as process color, an illustration is photographically "separated" into three colors (cyan, magenta, and yellow) plus black. Each color is reproduced on a separate printing plate, and the tiny dots from each plate are lined up, or registered, so as give a near-perfect reproduction of an illustration, with all the variety of tones and colors.

Process color allowed magazines to print pictures by re-nowned illustrators such as Maxfield Parrish, whose stunning work was featured on the covers of *Collier's*, *Ladies' Home Journal*, and other magazines. These illustrations were printed in a style called poster cover, which had no lines or type in the picture to detract from the beauty. Highly coveted by the public, poster cover magazines were often framed and hung in peoples' homes.

"To See and Be Shown"

Until the 1930s high-quality illustrations and photographs were used as adjuncts to magazine stories—they provided visuals to highlight the words in the articles. However, that concept changed when Henry Luce, powerful American publisher and editor of *Time*, bought *Life* magazine in 1936. Luce believed many Americans were undereducated and sought a new way to bring them the latest science news, current events, and human interest stories. To do so, he hired the best photographers in the business to tell stories a new way, through photojournalism, using pho-tographs rather than words to convey the news.

Life was printed in a large format on heavy white paper. The first is-sue featured a new type of graphic design. It contained fifty pages of pictures with short captions of text accompanying the photos. Although Luce only printed 380,000 copies of the first issue, within four months *Life* was selling over 1 million copies a week.

The new magazine format could not be ignored by publishers, and it

Cover of the first issue of *Life* magazine. *Life* was the first magazine to emphasize the importance of photos in its stories.

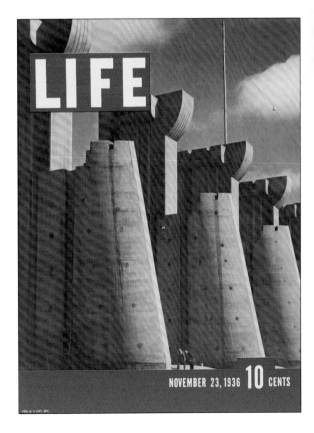

did not take long for others, including *Look*, the Paris *Match*, and the British *Picture Post* to imitate *Life*. These magazines created what was called a visual literacy among the public. People learned to spot good images and came to expect more than simple photos and articles in their magazines. As Luce noted, "To see life; to see the world; to eyewitness great events; to see strange things . . . to see man's work . . . to see and be amazed . . . to see and be shown is now the will and expectancy of half of mankind."[33]

"A Musical Feeling"

With magazines like *Life* raising expectations, many publishers realized they needed to enlist talented graphic arts professionals to design their pages. And the influence of these art directors is still felt today. One of the most revered graphic designers, Alexey Brodovitch, was hired as art director of *Harper's Bazaar* in 1934. He worked at the magazine for twenty-four years.

Brodovitch, a Russian émigré who had lived in Paris, sought to create a flowing experience for readers as they paged through the magazine. To give layouts a feeling of movement, type and images were laid out in varying sizes from page to page. To provide spontaneity, pages with complex, dense layouts were alternated with those containing simple designs surrounded by large areas of white space. This approach was associated with modernism, an art style typified by Dutch artist Piet Mondrian, who used bright boxes of color placed within thick black lines and surrounded by fields of white. This style was adopted by Brodovitch and other art directors to give magazines an elegant, modern look.

One observer stated that Brodovitch's magazine design techniques provided "a musical feeling, a rhythm resulting from the interaction of space and time. He and [editor] Carmel Snow would dance around the pages spread before them on the floor, trying to pick up the rhythm."[34]

Brodovitch's musical design work went beyond simple layouts of text, type, and pictures. In 1944 he hired photographer Richard Avedon, who set new standards for fashion photography. Rather than shoot models standing aloof and stationary,

Carmel Snow (seated at the desk) and Alexey Brodovitch (kneeling) look over the layout of *Harper's Bazaar,* 1952.

Avedon brought action and emotion to his pictures by shooting the models smiling, moving, and laughing. Meanwhile, Snow ensured that dull articles on clothes and accessories were intermixed with stories by respected women writers such as Virginia Woolf and Eudora Welty. Together Brodovitch and Snow provided *Harper's Bazaar* with a distinctive identity that stood out among the hundreds of magazines on a newsstand.

Brodovitch was relentless in his pursuit of graphic arts innovation, and he never stopped modernizing and changing the look of his magazines. His motto was "Make it new."[35]

The Golden Age of Magazine Design

Brodovitch's main competitor was Ukrainian-born designer Mehemed Fehmy Agha. Agha was known for his art direction of *House & Garden*, *Vogue*, and *Vanity Fair*, the latter of which bills itself as "the arts and culture showcase of America."[36] Agha pioneered the use of the double-page spread in *Vogue*, utilizing the two single pages of an open magazine as a large canvas on which to place a layout. This technique allowed the reproduction of big, bold photos and provided expansive feelings of depth for the reader. Agha also introduced the duotone, a method of printing halftones that uses only two colors and gives images a rich, antique look that implies durability and style. Another printing technique initiated by Agha, called bleed printing, eliminates white borders on a page with the ink "bleeding" off the edge of the paper.

Agha used top photographers like Edward Steichen, Edward Weston, and Louise Dahl-Wolfe and was the first to expose American magazine readers to the artwork of French impressionist painter Henri Matisse and other famed artists. Under Agha's direction, *Vanity Fair* introduced the first magazine cover with full-color photography in 1932.

The innovations put in place by Agha and Brodovitch spawned what design historian William Owen called a golden age of magazine design between 1945 and 1968. Many of the people who led this golden age had worked as photographers and art directors under Agha and Brodovitch. They were intent on giving their publications cutting-edge graphic designs that would separate them from the rest. And some of the pages featuring their groundbreaking layouts look as fresh today as they did in the 1950s and 1960s.

The New York Style

The art directors of the golden age belonged to what was called the New York style of design. Practitioners of the New York style were editorial and advertising designers who took the separate entities of text, photos, and illustrations and unified them into single visual statements.

At *McCall's*, art director and photographer Otto Storch linked type and photography in unique ways. For example, in an article titled "Why Mommy Can't Read," the words are written on a pair of glasses, but look bent and wavy, as if distorted by failing vision. For the article "The Forty-Winks Reducing Plan," a woman is shown sleeping on her side on a

MAXFIELD PARRISH

The ability to reproduce color illustrations cheaply in the early twentieth century set off competition among publishers to hire the best illustrators available. One of the most popular illustrators from this era, Maxfield Parrish, is known for his brightly colored illustrations of dreamlike landscapes occupied by scantily clad young men and women. These fantasies, with names like Ecstasy, Land of Make Believe, *and* Dream Castle in the Sky, *appeared in* Collier's, Good Housekeeping, Harper's, Ladies' Home Journal, Life, *and* Scribner.

Parrish is best known for his use of color, and he was keenly aware of color printing techniques used to reproduce his work on magazine pages. To achieve the best outcome, Parrish did not mix paint colors but worked with them directly as they came out of the tube. He then built up layers of paint using a glaze over each color before applying the next. Discussing his technique in 1950, Parrish compared it to process printing:

Well—this method is very simple. . . . It is somewhat like the modern reproductions in four-color half tone, where the various gradations are obtained by printing one color plate over another on a white ground of paper. . . . Colors are applied just as they come from the tube, the original purity and quality is never lost: a purple is pure . . . the quality of each is never [destroyed] by mixing . . . you are apt to get what is wanted, and have a richness and glow of one color shining through the other, not to be had by mixing.

Quoted in Jim Vadeboncoeur Jr., "Maxfield Parrish Biography," BPIB. www.bpib.com/illustrat/parrish.htm.

mattress, made of type. Her body causes sags in the mattress and the text of the article follows the curves of her body. Commenting on such novel ideas, Storch wrote in 1980: "I did not think that pictures and typography were an end in themselves, but just component parts of the message. . . . For me, idea, copy, art and typography became inseparable."[37]

In addition to articles, the New York style was seen in the advertisements that filled magazine pages. Gene Federico was one of the premiere advertising art directors and designers in the post–World War II era, recognized for his ability to push the boundaries of ad design.

Federico's specialty was typography. For example, a 1953 ad for *Woman's Day* shows a woman riding a bicycle. The wheels of the bike are two lowercase *o*'s in the Futura font that are part of the words "Go Out" in the headline "She's Got to Go Out to Get *Woman's Day*." Commenting on his style, Steven Heller wrote in the *New York Times*:

> At most agencies, copywriters dominated the creative side, with text segregated from images in unimaginative, cookie-cutter layouts. The art director was a mere functionary. . . . Federico, however . . . became one of a handful of contemporary advertising designers to develop a distinctly [modern] approach to graphic design. It emphasized clean layout, asymmetrical composition and sans-serif typefaces, and it was rooted in the often witty union of word and picture.[38]

Concept Advertising: "It's Like Love"

Federico was one of the first people to believe that humor could be used to sell a product. Today with so many funny or clever ads, it may be hard to understand that at one time advertisers did not like to associate their products with humor. That changed in the 1960s, when legendary advertising agency Doyle Dane Bernbach began taking what was called the concept approach to advertising.

Concept advertisers utilized a memorable catch phrase that was repeated in ads with different pictures, often to humorous results. For example, Doyle Dane Bernbach's first successful campaign for Levy's Rye Bread showed the words "You don't have to be Jewish to love Levy's" in a simple font. The words were placed with photos of various people, including an older Native American, an African American man, and a young Japanese boy all enjoying sandwiches on Levy's bread. Created by writer Judy Protas and art director Bill Taubin, the ads were an international hit and dramatically increased the sales of Levy's rye.

Other Doyle Dane Bernbach ads became cultural milestones in the 1960s. Their "Think Small" ads for the Volkswagen Beetle used graphic design to make a point. A small image of the VW was placed on the upper left corner of the page surrounded by a sea of white paper. Beneath, the words "Think Small" and some clever copy conveyed a simple, yet eye-catching and humorous message.

Many of the agency's daring designs are attributed to its founder, William Bernbach, who summarized his design philosophies with two memorable statements: "Rules are what the artist breaks; the memorable never emerged from a formula," and "Logic and over-analysis can immobilize and sterilize an idea. It's like love—the more you analyze it, the faster it disappears."[39]

Adbusters

Despite Bernbach's words, many business executives were analyzing ads and reaching the same conclusion—good design can sell products. This was happening during an era of hippies and antiwar protests, and advertisers quickly incorporated counterculture images into their ads. As former adman and founder of the magazine *Adbusters* Kalle Lasn writes:

> During the '60s, in the midst of one of the biggest cultural revolutions of our time, corporations discovered that cool could be incredibly profitable. While young people spontaneously took to the streets and organized festivals and anti-war protests, corporations started

raiding their counterculture for eye-catching signifiers and stylistic expressions to incorporate into their marketing campaigns. Thus began a two-step dance of authentic cool and fake, commercialized cool. . . . In one of the most stunning cultural coups d'état ever, ad agency gurus figured out how to . . . transform alienation and despair into consent.[40]

Driven by the success of these coordinated campaigns, advertisers sought to create total saturation for their products, putting their logos on nearly everything. As a result advertisements showed up everywhere in the decades that followed. In addition to their usual place on TV and radio, ads popped up on bus stops, automobiles, billboards, signboards, the walls of public restrooms, and even on T-shirts and caps bearing logos for designers.

By the mid-1990s the average American consumer living in a typical city was looking at over three thousand commercial

As advertising became more competitive, companies tried to saturate the market with their message in creative ways, such as these public restrooms sponsored by Charmin toilet paper.

messages each day. This was a result of more than $148 billion spent annually by the ad industry. Marketers increasingly aimed their ad campaigns at young people, and consumer spending continued to rise throughout the decade and into the twenty-first century. For advertisers the increased spending proved that their work was indeed very effective. However, this created a backlash among those who were tired of being bombarded by ads everywhere they went.

In Vancouver, Canada, Lasn and former advertising designer Bill Schmalz were so fed up with corporate ads that they founded *Adbusters* to refute the claims made by advertisers. According to the magazine's Web site, *Adbusters* is "the new social activist movement of the information age. Our aim is to topple existing power structures and forge a major shift in the way we will live in the 21st century."[41]

The people at *Adbusters* believe that people are assailed with ads everywhere they look. According to Lasn, "Since the second world war we have created a consumer culture pumping something like 3,000 to 5,000 messages into our brains every day [when you count logos on products] from the time you are a baby."[42] Lasn believes that this bombardment prevents people from thinking about the negative costs of consumer culture. For example, some of the most expensive designer brands are made by Chinese laborers in sweatshops where the working conditions border on slavery. In addition, there are dozens of environmental problems with mass-consumerism that add to global warming, air and water pollution, and depletion of natural resources.

To educate young consumers, *Adbusters* uses clever graphic designs to wage anticonsumer campaigns. These ads are called anti-ads, uncommercials, or subvertisements (subversive advertisements) and are created for culture jamming: that is, opposing the corporate advertising that dominates modern society. For example, *Adbusters* creates spoof ads that look like the expensive advertisements created for Marlboro, Calvin Klein, Budweiser, McDonald's, and others. "The True Colors of Benetton" ad makes fun of the famous "United Colors of Benetton" campaign with a picture that shows a man in a white shirt and tie with his mouth stuffed full of hundred dollar bills. A spoof on a Diesel ad shows a sexy young couple in a provocative pose on a billboard above a desolate city street in a poor neighborhood. The attitude of the people in the ad could not be more indifferent to the image of boarded-up store windows and feelings of despair generated by the picture.

Adbusters also wages a battle against consumerism with campaigns such as TV Turnoff Week and Buy Nothing Day. The poster for the November 2007 Buy Nothing campaign features a red frame with the word "Celebrate" on top. Large block letters in boxes of black and white say "BUY NOTHING DAY." In a bit of typographical illustration that would make Federico proud, the *A* in *DAY* is the uncapped pyramid with the all-seeing eye featured on the back of the one-dollar bill.

UNCOMMERCIALS AND SUBVERTISEMENTS

Kalle Lasn coined the phrase "culture jamming" to describe the methods Adbusters *uses, such as uncommercials and subvertisements, to oppose the slick advertising campaigns of big corporations. In his book* Culture Jam: How to Reverse America's Suicidal Consumer Binge—and Why We Must, *Lasn explains the* Adbusters *culture jam manifesto:*

We will take on the archetypal mind polluters and beat them at their own game. We will uncool their billion-dollar brands with uncommercials on TV, subvertisements in magazines and anti-ads right next to theirs in the urban landscape. We will seize control of the roles and functions that corporations play in our lives and set new agendas in their industries. We will jam the pop-culture marketeers and bring their image factory to a sudden, shuddering halt. On the rubble of the old culture, we will build a new one with a non-commercial heart and soul.

Quoted in "Culture Jamming," The Flying University, July 9, 2001. http://sg.geocities.com/theflyinguniversity/activism/jamming.htm.

The Buy Nothing Campaign generated media attention and some controversy. MTV refused to run the *Adbusters* commercial featuring another piece of graphics wizardry—a giant animated clay pig protruding from a map of North America. Despite the problems, *Adbusters* believes that at least half a million people participated in the campaign and bought nothing that day.

Ironically, the anti-advertising people have won a substantial number of awards for their graphic arts designs. The magazine is known for its design, which shocks through juxtaposition, or contrast between two elements, such as in the Diesel spoof. And as former employee of the magazine Guy Ryan Bigge writes, *Adbusters* "is now winning still more design awards for its filthy, chaotic, zine-like appearance."[43]

"A Vibrant and Healthy Medium"

Although *Adbusters* is one of the more unusual magazines to be published in the last century, it shares design features with *McCall's* of the 1960s and even *Harper's Bazaar* of the 1930s. Despite the latest software programs used to create *Adbusters*, its graphic artists are still placing text, type, sidebars, and other elements in ways long familiar to magazine designers. And in doing so, they help magazines retain a special place in modern culture and society. As Johnson and Prijatel write:

> Magazines . . . remain a vibrant and healthy medium, serving the rabble, the rebel, and responsible citizen. Magazines, in a way, are a voice of the country. They are published by huge media conglomerates and tiny publishing houses, by trade and religious groups, by professional associations, and by academics. They are created for thinkers, laborers, activists, and couch potatoes. Some are huge financial machines; others don't make a dime. Some need two city blocks to staff their offices, others need nothing more than a kitchen table. No other medium is as diverse, nor does any other medium have such a rich past and limitless future.[44]

5

A New Age of Design

During the first half of the twentieth century, graphic designers worked to communicate clearly and unambiguously. They used square lines, contrasting colors, and sans serif type so that the viewer would easily understand the message. This approach was associated with modernism and was adopted by art directors for periodicals and ad agencies during the golden era of magazine design.

By the early 1970s the clean, modernist approach began to break down when young designers rejected the rational communication style of mainstream art directors. The new generation, raised during the psychedelic 1960s, sought to put their own individual stamp on designs, rather than adhere to established rules. This signaled the beginning of what art historians call the postmodern or new-wave era. As R. Roger Remington explains in *American Modernism: Graphic Design, 1920–1960*: "Designers questioned the need for functionality in graphic design. They preferred solutions that most often were personal expressions involving complexity, subjectivity, and ambiguity."[45]

Subjectivity, or interpreting something based on personal opinions, was not an option available to earlier graphic designers. Nor was ambiguity, or expressing something in a vague or uncertain way. However, there were several factors at work that sounded the death knell for modernist design in the 1970s. It was an era when women, minorities, and immigrants were playing a more essential role in advertising and design for the first time. The newcomers challenged the way things were done while at the same time introducing fresh sensibilities and creativity to a field that had largely been dominated by white males.

Another aspect shook graphics tradition in the mid-1970s, when angry young musicians and artists called punks burst onto the scene in London and New York. As designer Richard Hollis describes the movement in *Graphic Design: A Concise History*, "Punk, in its most obvious form, was a . . . street style, part of a culture of drugs and pop music, rebellious with a desire to shock."[46]

Punk graphic artists created fanzines, also called 'zines, which were homemade music magazines about popular punk bands. The 'zines used scribbled words, crude drawings, and letters and pictures torn out of popular magazines—what Hollis calls "anti-Design."[47] In an era before personal computers, punks reproduced fanzines with lithography and photocopy machines. While the reach of the fanzines was limited, the punk style of graphic design reached a larger audience in 1977 on a record cover of the punk band the Sex Pistols, whose album *God Save the Queen* was an international hit.

Energetic Expression

The rise of fanzines was aided by technology that gave graphic artists greater control over the production process. The photomechanical transfer, or PMT, camera is a large machine that looks like a giant enlarger and is used in photography darkrooms. The machine, introduced around 1970, transfers photographs, illustrations, or type into high-contrast black-and-white reproductions called photostats. It can also be used to enlarge or reduce images to fit into layouts. With PMTs, graphic artists could produce complete finished layouts, or camera-ready art, instead of giving detailed instructions to typesetters and halftone makers. In this way, the PMT process allowed the new generation of designers to put their personal stamp on each and every layout.

While most graphic artists used PMTs to produce clean layouts, German-born designer Wolfgang Weingart went to extremes in Switzerland. Feeling that the refined modernist style had become stodgy and bland, Weingart began challenging accepted design rules in the late 1960s. By the mid-1970s he had helped create the new-wave style, which abandoned stark, organized modernism in favor of wide letter spacing and the tendency to change fonts, sizes, and letter weights (such as bold or narrow) in a single word. This style was combined with visual collages in which Weingart created a single layout with photographs, photographic negatives, overlapping images, numbers, arrows, boxes of type, and cartoon balloons filled with words.

Terry Jones, a former editor of *Vogue*, followed a similar path in 1980 with his fanzine *i-D*. According to Hollis, the magazine "was the most energetic expression of every kind of new technology, which it used by abusing it—enormously

The cover of the Sex Pistols album *God Save the Queen* featured the punk style of graphic design.

enlarged photocopies and copies distorted by moving the paper, Polaroid instant photographs over- or under-exposed and scratched or painted on."[48]

Digital Wit and Style

Soon after Jones created his punk magazine, designers had new tools at their disposal. Digital word-processing programs were first introduced in the late 1970s, but the digital revolution in graphics did not begin until Apple introduced its Macintosh computer in 1984. This machine allowed designers, for the first time, to create numerous type fonts in various sizes and manipulate and organize text, photos, and images on a computer monitor.

The fonts and icons used on the early Macs were created by designer Susan Kare and are familiar to countless millions today. Kare designed the Happy Mac face that appears when the machine is booted up and invented the "command" symbol on Mac keyboards. She also created the wristwatch that appears when the machine is performing time-consuming functions; the hand icon that pushes pages up and down; the document folder suitcase; the trash can; and the dreaded bomb with a lit fuse that appears when a computer crashes. In addition, Kare designed the tool icons called the Lasso, the Grabber, and the Paint Bucket for the first painting and illustration software programs, MacPaint and MacDraw.

Kare had to ensure that her icons would be understood by people on every continent. And the earliest Mac operating systems were only 400 kB in size—a modern three-minute MP3 file is more than ten times bigger. Therefore, Kare's designs had to use very few pixels, that is, the dots on the screen that generate images. To help her achieve this task, Kare studied ancient mosaics, pictures made of small pieces of colored tile or glass.

Some of Kare's designs were retired when Apple created OS X (operating system 10) in 2000. But according to the Museum of Modern Art in New York, Kare is "a pioneering and influential computer iconographer. . . . Using a minimalist grid of pixels and constructed with mosaic-like precision, her icons communicate their function immediately and memorably, with wit and style."[49]

Kare continues to change with the times. In recent years she has been designing icons for the popular social networking Web site Facebook. Her gift applications such as puppies, cupcakes, teddy bears, and roses allow users to send virtual gifts to one another.

A Virtual Landscape

The introduction of the computer sent shock waves through the graphic arts world. As the American Institute of Graphic Arts Web site states, "Most designers were skeptical of—if not completely opposed to—the idea of integrating the computer into design practice, perhaps fearing an uncertain future wherein the tactility [sensitivity] of the hand was usurped by the mechanics of bits and bytes."[50] However, with a computer's ability to integrate graphic design, typesetting, photo reproduction, and printing functions, most designers could not ignore the new technology. Design schools were required to change their curricula, and art directors were forced to learn to work with unfamiliar and often quirky machines. And designers such as April Greiman were able to use this new tool in ways that changed the visual design world forever.

Los Angeles–based Greiman was one of the first graphic artists to recognize the potential of the early Macs. Having studied with Weingart, she experimented with ways to bring a new-wave sensibility to a digital format. Her first attempt, a poster called *Iris Light*, was created when Greiman shot a traditional film photograph of an image on a video monitor. Discussing the piece that was a hybrid of old and new technologies, Greiman said of the image, "Instead of looking like a bad photograph, the image . . . looked like a painting; it captured the spirit of light."[51]

Greiman found new ways to incorporate unusual digital techniques in 1986 when she was asked to contribute to an issue of *Design Quarterly*. Upon taking the assignment, Greiman understood that it was the responsibility of a postmodern designer to question accepted concepts. In her contribution she challenged the idea of what a magazine is supposed to be, as the title of the project, *Does It Make Sense?* suggests. Although she was commissioned to create thirty-two pages of designs, Greiman discarded the notion of a typical magazine layout. Instead,

THE POSTMODERN ERA

The last quarter of the twentieth century is known as the postmodern era. In A History of Graphic Design, communications professor Philip B. Meggs explains postmodernism and the motivating forces behind it:

By the 1970s, many people believed the modern era was drawing to a close in art, design, politics, and literature. The cultural norms of Western society were scrutinized and the authority of traditional institutions was questioned. An era of pluralism emerged as people began to dispute the underlying tenets of modernism. The continuing quest for equality by women and minorities contributed to a growing climate of cultural diversity, as did immigration, international travel, and global communications. Accepted viewpoints were challenged by those who sought to remedy bias, prejudice, and distortion in the historical record. The social, economic, and environmental awareness of the period caused many to believe the modern aesthetic was no longer relevant in an emerging postindustrial society. People in many fields—including architects, economists, feminists, and even theologians—embraced the term *postmodernism* to express a climate of cultural change. Maddeningly vague and overused, *postmodernism* became a byword in the last quarter of the twentieth century.

In design, postmodernism designated the work of architects and designers who were breaking with the international style so prevalent since the [1930s]. Postmodernism sent shock waves through the design establishment as it challenged the order and clarity of modern design, particularly corporate design. . . . Perhaps the international style had been so thoroughly refined, explored, and accepted that a backlash was inevitable.

Philip B. Meggs, *A History of Graphic Design.* New York: Wiley, 1998, p. 432.

Does It Make Sense? was a pullout poster that was nearly 3 by 6 feet (.9 by 1.8m). The image on the poster was a digital collage of Greiman's nude body overlaid with low-resolution images of a dinosaur, the earth from the surface of the moon, and random text and drawings. An article about Greiman on the American Institute of Graphic Arts Web site describes the work:

> [Colorful] atmospheric . . . video images are interspersed with thoughtful comments and painstaking notations on the digital process—a virtual landscape of text and image. . . . The process of integrating digitized video images and [computerized] type was not unlike pulling teeth in the early days of Macintosh and MacDraw. The files were so large, and the equipment so slow that she would send the file to print when she left the studio in the evening and it would just be finished when she returned in the morning.[52]

Greiman also used MacDraw to cut and paste various parts of her body, demonstrating largely unrecognized abilities of digital equipment. Although her poster was controversial at the time, her style came to be known as California new wave. Today such images are seen everywhere in advertisements, video graphics, and magazine articles.

In later years Greiman continued to make lasting contributions to the world of graphic design. Her posters such as the 1987 *Pacific Wave, Fortuny Museum*, the 1993 *AIGA Communication Graphics*, and the 2004 *Cal State Sacramento—Think About What You Think About* are outstanding examples of postmodern visual communication. And Greiman also challenged accepted forms of language. In 1984, when CalArts invited her to direct its graphic design program, she changed the department name to Visual Communications. Like earlier methods of production, Greiman felt that the term "graphic design" was too limiting for this exciting field.

"Hip as Rock & Roll"

Advances in software and digital technology continued to expand the abilities of graphic artists throughout the late 1980s.

Within the image:

Snow White
+ the Seven Pixels

Designer-In-Residence Program

An evening with April Greiman
presented as part of The Art Litho

Visual Presentation
8:00 pm
Thursday, November 6
1986
Maryland Institute
College of Art

Mount Royal Station Auditorium
Mount Royal Avenue + Cathedral Street

Reception following the lecture
in the Decker Gallery

Seating is unreserved.

An April Greiman design *Snow White and the Seven Pixels.* Greiman was one of the first designers to recognize the potential of the computer in graphic design.

For example, the page-design application QuarkXPress, first introduced in 1987, allowed designers to place elements on a page with unprecedented precision and accuracy. This software, which was steadily updated in the early 1990s, was soon in widespread use by graphic artists, page designers, typesetters, and printers. In the early 1990s, David Carson utilized this advanced software to astonish the design community with a new breed of magazine that was as original as it was unreadable.

Carson, a former professional surfer, became a graphic designer in the late 1980s. As the art director for *Beach Culture*, *Surfer*, and *Ray Gun* between 1989 and 1996, Carson discarded magazine design rules in which text and images were laid out in a traditional grid pattern of columns, margins, and photo borders. Instead, he favored unlimited visual expression in the form of upside-down or backward type, wavy lines of text that might slump off the bottom of the page, several type fonts within a single paragraph, and sentences completely obscured with illustrations or other sentences laid over them in a different color. Letters could be sliced off and sentences might be incomplete, which invited the reader to fill in his or her own ideas.

In one issue of *Surfer*, Carson created confusing, out-of-sequence page numbers that were larger than the headlines of the articles. In *Ray Gun* he used single lines of text on a double page spread, extending across two pages. On another occasion, he ran two separate articles intermixed with one another to create a confusing jumble that required extreme patience from the reader trying to make sense of the words.

Carson was also famous for his odd photographic reproductions. A photo of country singer Lyle Lovett showed only his bare feet. For an issue featuring the rap group Beastie Boys, the cover was left blank except for the top two inches, which displayed a photo of the group. Carson explained that this was the only part of the magazine that shoppers at a magazine stand would see anyway. Carson also printed humorous, weird, and bizarre photos and illustrations sent in by subscribers, eliminating the distance between professional and amateur designers. Like the text, these might be printed upside down, as negative images, or sliced and diced to fit into layouts. In *The End of Print: The Graphic Design of David Carson*, musician David Byrne of the band Talking Heads describes Carson's extreme graphics as "beautiful, radical, impractical design of and by the people . . . hip as Rock & Roll."[53]

Oddly, although Carson is associated with the computer design revolution, many of his most innovative designs were created as traditional, old-style camera-ready art laid out on cardboard. Whatever the case, his groundbreaking work shook

The introduction of Macintosh computers in 1984 changed graphic design forever. The machines were developed with the needs of artists in mind, and several types of early Macintosh software revolutionized visual communication. One of the earliest programs, MacPaint, by computer programmer Bill Atkinson and graphic designer Susan Kare, had a groundbreaking human interface in which the tool icons controlled by the newly invented mouse or graphics tablet enabled designers to digitize their ideas easily and naturally.

In 1985 Macintosh began selling its computers with Adobe PostScript. This software sent text, images, and graphic elements to the Apple LaserWriter printer. Another piece of software, Aldus PageMaker, allowed graphic artists to pick fonts, type sizes, page margins, borders, and other elements.

Together with the Macintosh computer, the software created a new field called desktop publishing, or DTS. People could now combine text and images on a computer for use in publishing books, magazines, advertisements, and creative projects. This saved a great deal of money and time for those who worked to prepare pages for printing. Today desktop publishing is a multibillion-dollar business, and nearly every graphic artist uses a computer for visual communications.

up the world of graphics. Although it was condemned by professionals, it was beloved by a younger generation raised not on magazines but on the frenetic images of music videos.

Redesigning Type

While Carson's work was on the cutting edge of visual communication, a new generation of typographers began using computers to design typefaces. They created an explosion of new fonts in the early 1990s unparalleled in graphic arts history.

At Adobe, calligrapher and mathematician Sumner Stone worked with Carol Twombly and Robert Slimbach to create the typographic program called Adobe Originals. These high-quality fonts, such as Utopia, Lithos, and Adobe's version of the classic Caslon, were used by desktop publishers in countless designs. Meanwhile, Apple designers created another version of Garamond, a narrower rendering of the serif typeface created in the sixteenth century. Apple used this font, called ITC Garamond, with its classic Apple corporate logo and with its popular 1997 "Think Different" advertising campaign. However, many typographers criticized Apple's ITC Garamond, calling it a poorly designed takeoff of the classic style and "Garamond" in name only. Despite the criticism, the font was seen by perhaps billions of people in the 1990s. In 2002 Apple took another font, Myriad, designed for Adobe by Slimbach and Twombly, and created its own version for advertising and packaging. Called Myriad Apple, the sans serif font was used on the early iPods and also used to market the portable media players.

"Raucously Artful" Type

Beyond the major corporations, countless type designers were empowered by the computer to create their own studios, called type foundries, a term dating back to the early years of printing when type was forged from hot metal. Of the more successful type foundries, Emigre Graphics of Berkeley, California, was among the first to take advantage of the typographic potential of Macintosh computers in the mid-1980s. In an interview with British journalist Rhonda Rubinstein, Emigre founder Zuzana Licko describes the unique possibilities she saw in the Mac:

> The Macintosh . . . was a relatively crude tool back then, so established designers looked upon it as a cute novelty. But to me it seemed as wondrously uncharted as my fledgling design career. It was a fortunate coincidence; I'm sure that being free of preconceived notions regarding typeface design helped me in exploring this new medium to the fullest. . . . It has continued to be the ideal tool for me.[54]

FONTISM

Before the mid-1980s the word font *was virtually unknown by the general public. In* Graphic Style: From Victorian to Digital, *Steven Heller and Seymour Chwast explain how the computer revolutionized typographic design and introduced "fontism" to the world:*

Of all the terms to emerge from the graphic arts during the personal computer era, "font" (originally signifying a unified set of hot metal letters, which precedes the digital epoch by centuries) has been most integrated into the mass culture. Your average computer user talks of fonts as though the word was never arcane professional jargon. The reason is that software for the Macintosh and PC democratized both the use and manufacture of type. Until the advent of the computer, type creation was the sole province of skilled draftsmen, punch-cutters, and letterform designers who toiled at perfecting every nuance of a particular alphabet. The process could take months, even years. Yet during the nineties, programs like Fontographer enabled craftsmen and neophytes to create type. Both contributed to new methods and aesthetics practiced today. Graphic designers and artists saw type as another expressively interpretative medium. Without the strictures imposed by tradition, designers did not follow the same rules that had always governed production. Type no longer had to be pristine or legible, as long as it evoked a mood, established an aura, or signaled a code. Weird, quirky, and discordant typo-imagery, similar to early twentieth-century Cubist painting, developed into a raucous, layered graphic style.

Steven Heller and Seymour Chwast, *Graphic Style: From Victorian to Digital.* New York: Abrams, 2000, p. 241.

In the years that followed, Licko and other Emigre designers created controversy with eccentric fonts such as Dead History, Exocet, Keedy Sans, Remedy, and Totally Gothic. Although some challenged the experimental look of the type, unusual Emigre fonts were seen in major advertising campaigns and publication designs. In addition, the foundry published the graphic design magazine *Emigre* for twenty-one years, from 1984 to 2005.

Emigre was one of the first major publications produced on a Macintosh, and its innovative and outspoken articles were extremely influential within the visual communications industry. Describing the antimodernist style of the magazine, Steven Heller and Seymour Chwast write in *Graphic Style: From Victorian to Digital*:

> The tabloid-sized quarterly defied the tenets of Modern layout much in the same way that sixties Psychedelic poster artists upended the rules of legibility—laying down rules of their own. Under Modernism, type had become a neutral frame within which crisp and clean photographs or abstract illustrations were composed. *Emigre* was typocentric. Its typography was its content. By eradicating any semblance of the Modernist grid, [*Emigre* magazine founder Rudy] VanderLans opened up the printed page to unfettered, raucously artful typographic configurations.[55]

The art seen in *Emigre* pushed the boundaries of accepted ideas about graphic arts. But in the big money world of advertising, corporations still needed their ads to clearly sell products even while they projected a hip, cool image. This resulted in advertising designs Heller and Chwast describe as "controlled chaos."[56] The ads incorporated some of the unusual techniques pioneered by Emigre and Carson, such as oddly cropped photos and mixed font sizes and styles. But the layouts remained readable enough to convey the advertiser's message, which not only sold a product but purportedly presented the corporation as sharing common values with the young, cutting-edge MTV generation.

A New Narrative

Even as art directors were redrawing the rule books, graphic design entered a new era with the advent of the Internet. Although it is difficult for many to remember today, the general public barely knew of the Internet in 1993, when the Mosaic Web browser was first introduced. However, beginning in 1994 public use of the World Wide Web doubled annually, leaving corporations scrambling to create their own Web sites. By 1997 new Web addresses were being created at a rate of one per minute, and there were an estimated 150 million Web pages online—that number had topped 1 billion by 2000.

Unlike books and magazines, Web sites incorporate not only text and images but sounds, video, and animation. Graphic artists who transformed into Web designers could no longer think of making individual page layouts but had to create interconnected Web sites that incorporated pages connected by hyperlinks (highlighted words, icons, or images coded to link to other Web pages).

Designs could be three-dimensional, such as rotating cubes with information on each side. Or they could be "point-and-click" sites where various parts of an image led to different Web sites. Web design was only limited by imagination. Those schooled in the controlled chaos of the late 1980s and early 1990s had a natural advantage.

Technology today allows virtually anyone to design a Web site.

One of those designers, Jessica Helfand, set the standard for what was to follow when her agency produced Discovery Channel Online in 1994. In creating the site, Helfand and design director William Drenttel sought to achieve three goals—presenting a memorable identity for the channel, allowing easy navigation through the site, and giving a clear, organized presentation of its TV programs. To achieve these goals, the designers had to consider new elements unfamiliar to most graphic artists, as the Jessica Helfand/William Drenttel Web site explains:

> Discovery Channel Online was designed to evolve in complexity as the (then-new) technology grew to support it. Combining daily story postings, programming highlights, interactive games and great storytelling . . . it was designed to embrace new narrative opportunities: shorter, non-scrolling text screens, hyperlinks edited for brevity [shortness] and impact, and images optimized for fast downloading.[57]

The Discovery Channel site was very influential and set the standard for interactive designs in the 1990s. And as Helfand understood, technology continued to evolve and support new applications. By 2000 the integration of motion graphics, animation, video feeds, and music into Web site design created a fusion between the traditional print media, broadcast television, and movies. This expansion added yet another dimension to graphic design that was unthinkable as recently as the early 1990s.

A parallel revolution has taken place outside of the world of professional designers. Software such as Adobe Dreamweaver, introduced in 1997, allows skilled amateurs to design their own complex, interactive Web sites. And in more recent years, Web development software has become extremely user-friendly. Today nearly anyone with computer skills can download freeware (free software) to create their own Web sites. As a result, countless millions have become Internet graphic designers. Their Web sites deliver stories, art, music, movies, product information, and educational materials to a worldwide audience.

Just as Gutenberg's press brought communication to the masses in the fifteenth century, the Internet allows people from any region of the globe to reach out to a mass audience. And since the ancient Egyptians directed their kings to heaven by combining words and images on papyrus, graphic artists have played a major role in helping the human race in its quest for interaction and communication.

Notes

Chapter 1: Everyday Art

1. United States Department of the Treasury, "FAQs: Currency." www.us treas.gov/education/faq/currency/por traits.shtml#q3.
2. "Heraldry & the Parts of a Coat of Arms," Fleur-de-lis Designs. www.fleu rdelis.com/coatofarms.htm.
3. LearnAboutHandbags.com, "Mono-grammed Purses." www.learnabouth andbags.com/monogrammed-purses .html.
4. Herbert Bayer et al., *Seven Designers Look at Trademark Design*. Chicago: Theobald, 1952, p. 50.
5. Quoted in Charlotte Jirousek, "The Arts and Crafts Movement," Art, Design, and Visual Thinking. http:// char.txa.cornell.edu/art/decart/art craft/artcraft.htm.
6. Jeremy Aynsley, *A Century of Graphic Design*. Hauppauge, NY: Barron's Educational Series, 2001, p. 16.
7. Aynsley, *A Century of Graphic Design*, p. 16.
8. Quoted in Official Web Site of Raymond Loewy, "About: Biography." www.raymondloewy.com/about/bio2 .html.
9. Quoted in Official Web Site of Raymond Loewy, "About: Biography."

Chapter 2: Book Arts

10. Norma Levarie, *The Art and History of Books*. Newcastle, DE: Oak Knoll, 1995, p. 60.
11. Stephen Fry, "The Medieval Season," BBC. www.bbc.co.uk/bbcfour/medi eval/gutenberg.shtml.
12. Quoted in Nicole Howard, *The Book*. Westport, CT: Greenwood, 2005, p. 32.
13. Quoted in Michel Wlassikoff, *The Story of Graphic Design in France*. Corte Madre, CA: Gingko, 2005, p. 17.
14. Quoted in Richard Hollis, *Graphic Design: A Concise History*. London: Thames & Hudson, 2001, p. 55.

Chapter 3: The Art of the Poster

15. Quoted in Ebria Feinblatt and Bruce Davis, *Toulouse-Lautrec and His Contemporaries: Posters of the Belle Epoque*. Los Angeles: Los Angeles County Museum of Art, 1985, p. 10.
16. Alois Senefelder, "The Invention of Lithography," University of Georgia Libraries, March 15, 2006. http:// fax.libs.uga.edu/NE2420xS475/1f/ invention_of_lithography.txt.
17. Philip B. Meggs, *A History of Graphic Design*. New York: Wiley, 1998, p. 185.

18. Meggs, *A History of Graphic Design*, pp. 185–86.
19. Feinblatt and Davis, *Toulouse-Lautrec and His Contemporaries*, p. 14.
20. Quoted in Feinblatt and Davis, *Toulouse-Lautrec and His Contemporaries*, p. 16.
21. Meggs, *A History of Graphic Design*, p. 183.
22. Quoted in Meggs, *A History of Graphic Design*, p. 251.
23. Quoted in Hollis, *Graphic Design*, p. 33.
24. Quoted in Therese Heyman, "Posters American Style: Patriotic Persuasion," Smithsonian American Art Museum. http://nmaa-ryder.si.edu/collections/exhibits/posters/objects/pp-noframe.html?/collections/exhibits/posters/objects/PP-1995.84.57_.html.
25. Heyman, "Posters American Style."
26. Northwestern University Library, "The World War II Poster Collection." www.library.northwestern.edu/govinfo/collections/wwii-posters/background.html.
27. Quoted in National Archives, "Powers of Persuasion." www.archives.gov/exhibits/powers_of_persuasion/its_a_womans_war_too/its_a_womans_war_too.html.
28. National Archives, "Powers of Persuasion."
29. Quoted in Joel Selvin, "Alton Kelley, Psychedelic Poster Creator, Dies," *San Francisco Chronicle*, June 3, 2008. www.sfgate.com/cgi-bin/article.cgi?f=/c/a/2008/06/03/BAQS111UJ4.DTL.
30. Meggs, *A History of Graphic Design*, p. 404.

Chapter 4: Designing for the Masses

31. Quoted in Ellen Mazur Thomson, *The Origins of Graphic Design in America, 1870–1920*. New Haven, CT: Yale University Press, 1997, p. 82.
32. Sammye Johnson and Patricia Prijatel, *The Magazine from Cover to Cover*. New York: Oxford University Press, 2007, p. 79.
33. Quoted in Mitchell Beazley, *Magazine Covers*. London: Octopus, 2006, p. 57.
34. Quoted in Johnson and Prijatel, *The Magazine from Cover to Cover*, p. 80.
35. Quoted in Johnson and Prijatel, *The Magazine from Cover to Cover*, p. 257.
36. Quoted in Design Archive Online, "Dr. Mehemed Fehmy Agha." http://design.rit.edu/biographies/agha.html.
37. Quoted in The Art Directors Club, "1980 Hall of Fame." www.adcglobal.org/archive/hof/1980/?id=262.
38. Steven Heller, "Gene Federico, 81, Graphic Designer, Dies," *New York Times*, September 10, 1999. http://query.nytimes.com/gst/fullpage.html?res=9E0CEFDB153DF933A2575AC0A96F958260.
39. Quoted in The Advertising Century, "William Bernbach." http://adage.com/century/people001.html.
40. Kalle Lasn, "The Reconquest of Cool," *Adbusters*, March 24, 2008. www.adbusters.org/magazine/76/The_Reconquest_of_Cool.html.
41. Adbusters, "About Adbusters." www.adbusters.org/about/adbusters.

42. Quoted in Andrew C. Revkin, "A Fresh Advertising Pitch: Buy Nothing," *New York Times*, November 22, 2007. http://dotearth.blogs.nytimes.com/2007/11/22/a-fresh-advertising-pitch-buy-nothing.

43. Guy Ryan Bigge, "The Bigge Idea," Blogspot, August 29, 2003. http://thebiggeidea.blogspot.com/2003_08_01_archive.html.

44. Johnson and Prijatel, *The Magazine from Cover to Cover*, p. 4.

Chapter 5: A New Age of Design

45. R. Roger Remington, *American Modernism: Graphic Design, 1920–1960*. New Haven, CT: Yale University Press, 2003, p. 169.

46. Hollis, *Graphic Design*, p. 188.

47. Hollis, *Graphic Design*, p. 188.

48. Hollis, *Graphic Design*, p. 191.

49. Quoted in "About," Susan Kare—User Interface Graphics. http://kare.com/about/bio.html.

50. American Institute of Graphic Arts, "April Greiman." www.aiga.org/content.cfm/medalist-aprilgreiman.

51. Quoted in American Institute of Graphic Arts, "April Greiman."

52. American Institute of Graphic Arts, "April Greiman."

53. Quoted in Lewis Blackwell and David Carson, *The End of Print: The Graphic Design of David Carson*. San Francisco: Chronicle, 1995, p. 7.

54. Quoted in Rhonda Rubinstein, "Emigre Fonts: Interview with Zuzana Licko," *Eye*, 2002. www.emigre.com/Licko.php.

55. Steven Heller and Seymour Chwast, *Graphic Style: From Victorian to Digital*. New York: Abrams, 2000, p. 235.

56. Heller and Chwast, *Graphic Style*, p. 244.

57. Jessica Helfand/William Drenttel, "Interactive." www.jhwd.com/indiscov.html.

Glossary

aesthetic: Pleasing in appearance.

fanzines: Homemade music magazines about popular bands with graphics that might include scribbled words, crude drawings, and torn-out letters and pictures clipped from magazines.

font: A complete set of letters, numbers, and punctuation of a particular typeface in which the individual characters have a similar design or style.

halftone: A method of reproducing a photo or illustration by rephotographing the image through a dot screen, which reduces the image to dots of various sizes.

intaglio: A printing method in which a design is cut or incised into a copper plate.

interlinear: Graphic design in which pictures are inserted between lines of text in a book or manuscript.

lithography: A method of printing in which an image is drawn on a flat stone with a grease pencil and transferred to paper.

logo: An easily recognized design or emblem used by a company on its letterhead, advertising, and products to provide a corporate identity.

pictograph or **pictogram:** A graphic symbol or picture that represents a word or idea.

serifs: Short decorative strokes added to letters. Typefaces without serifs are called sans serif.

typeface: A set of printed characters with a distinctive style, such as Garamond.

typographer: A person who designs typefaces and prepares type for printing.

For Further Reading

Books

Lewis Blackwell and David Carson, *The End of Print: The Graphic Design of David Carson*. San Francisco: Chronicle, 1995. A book filled with the cluttered postmodern graphics from Carson's groundbreaking magazines *Beach Culture*, *Surfer*, and *Ray Gun*.

Tamsin Blanchard, *Fashion and Graphics*. London: Laurence King, 2004. This book explores the packaging that makes fashion sell, putting the spotlight on the graphic designers who mold brand images from labels to shopping bags.

Nicole Howard, *The Book*. Westport, CT: Greenwood, 2005. An overview of the book's development across centuries and cultures, with discussions on the development of book materials, bindings, typefaces, and printing methods.

Philip B. Meggs, *A History of Graphic Design*. New York: Wiley, 2005. A definitive history of graphic communication with more than a thousand vivid illustrations that chronicle the fascinating quest to give visual form to ideas.

Lewann Sotnak, *Graphic Designer*. Mankato, MN: Capstone, 2000. An introduction to the career of graphic designer, including discussions of educational requirements, duties, workplace, salary, employment outlook, and possible future positions.

Web Sites

Adbusters (www.adbusters.org). Adbusters is a nonprofit magazine and Web site concerned about the powerful influence that commercial interests hold over the cultural environment. The magazine parodies slick corporate ads and challenges claims made by advertisers addressing issues ranging from genetically modified foods to media concentration.

The Advertising Century (http://adage.com/century/index.html). A site created in 1999 by *Advertising Age* in order to chronicle the ads that became a major cultural force and helped shape the identity of American society in the twentieth century.

Antiwar Cartoons and Political Parodies, About.com (http://political humor.about.com/library/images/blantiwarpics.htm). A collection of antiwar graphics, remixed propaganda posters, and other parody art expressing political dissent.

Font Diner (www.fontdiner.com/main.html). A Web site featuring unique and amusing font designs, with graphics reminiscent of a 1950s diner.

Nuremberg Chronicle, Beloit College (www.beloit.edu/nuremberg/index.htm). This site contains extensive information about the layout, design, and history of the famous fifteenth-century block book, along with hundreds of pages from it.

The Official Alphonse Mucha Web Site (www.muchafoundation.org/MHome.aspx). A site featuring the artwork and biography of the world-famous graphic designer.

Official Web Site of Raymond Loewy (www.raymondloewy.com). This Web site is maintained to honor the life, legend, and career of product designer Raymond Loewy and includes quotes, photos, awards, and career highlights of the renowned graphic artist.

Posters American Style: About Posters, Smithsonian Museum of American Art (http://nmaa-ryder.si.edu/collections/exhibits/posters/essay.html). Over a hundred American posters created for advertisements, wartime propaganda, rock bands, and public-information campaigns, with biographical information about the illustrators and comments about the designs.

Index

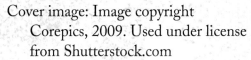

Picture Credits

Cover image: Image copyright Corepics, 2009. Used under license from Shutterstock.com

After Francis Barraud/The Bridgeman Art Library/Getty Images, 22

The Art Archive/Musée de l'Affiche Paris/Gianni Dagli Orti/The Picture Desk, Inc., 53

Art Resource, NY, 29

Bildarchiv Preussischer Kulturbesitz/ Art Resource, NY, 35, 50

Collection of the Norman Rockwell Museum at Stockbridge, Norman Rockwell Art Collection Trust, 68

© Corbis, 40

© David Crausby/Alamy, 84

© Robert Estall/Corbis, 45

© David R. Frazier Photolibrary, Inc./ Alamy, 95

Lewis W. Hine/George Eastman House/Getty Images, 41

HIP/Art Resource, NY, 31, 34

Image copyright Lisa Fischer, 2009. Used under license from Shutterstock.com, 64

Image copyright Terrance Emerson, 2009. Used under license from Shutterstock.com, 15

Image copyright zentilia, 2009. Used under license from Shutterstock .com, 12

Erich Lessing/Art Resource, NY, 38, 55

The Library of Congress, 58

© John McKenna/Alamy, 18

© The Museum of Modern Art/ Licensed by SCALA/Art Resource, NY, 63, 89

© The National Archives/Corbis, 60

The New York Public Library/Art Resource, NY, 70

Photo by Margaret Bourke-White/ Time and Life Pictures/Getty Images, 71

Spencer Platt/Getty Images, 78

Raymond Loewy™/® by CMG Worldwide, Inc./www.Raymond Loewy.com, 26

David Roth/Riser/Getty Images, 13

Walter Sanders/Time Life Pictures/ Getty Images, 73

Stephen Shugerman/Getty Images, 9

Wilson, Wes (b.1937)/Private Collection/The Bridgeman Art Library, 61

About the Author

Stuart A. Kallen is the prolific author of more than 250 nonfiction books for children and young adults. He has written on topics ranging from the theory of relativity to the history of world music. In addition, Kallen has written award-winning children's videos and television scripts. In his spare time, he is a singer/songwriter/guitarist in San Diego, California.